You Light Up Up
My Life

RB 1

Order this book online at www.trafford.com
or email orders@trafford.com

Most Trafford titles are also available at major online book retailers.

Printed in the United States of America.

ISBN: 978-1-4269-3780-4 (soft)
ISBN: 978-1-4269-3781-1 (ebook)

*Our mission is to efficiently provide the world's finest, most comprehensive
book publishing service, enabling every author to experience success.
To find out how to publish your book, your way, and have it available
worldwide, visit us online at www.trafford.com*

Trafford rev. 6/30/2010

 www.trafford.com

North America & international
toll-free: 1 888 232 4444 (USA & Canada)
phone: 250 383 6864 ♦ fax: 812 355 4082

CHAPTER 1

Sitting there worrying about the bills, how she was going to pay for them, where she would go if they didn't get paid was simply getting her nowhere fast. What she needed was an action plan. Now, the question was how was she to initiate some type of action plan if she didn't have the funds. Think….think…think….

If only she hadn't been so stupid as to trust that things would work out. That her husband was going to pick up the pieces and the pace when she had quit her job. Now, that was going right back to where she was before. Stop with the recriminations! Start with a more positive attitude! Well, she had been able to sustain the bills for some time. She had received that small government contract hadn't she? She could do something else with her assets. She just had to set her mind to finding that solution! And fast!

Well, the possibilities were endless. The question was what she had that was valuable and how was it possible to get the most out of it as possible. First, she needed to accurately address what she had, what was outstanding, and what was incoming. After completing this assessment, it appeared that the two largest outstanding balances were the mortgage and Stanford's credit card expenses. Since Stanford had amassed such large credit card balances, it seemed the most logical was to get rid of Stanford. Too bad her heart was unable to wrap herself around that solution.

Next, then was to negotiate with the credit card companies to prevent any future charges on these credit cards and a payoff plan that was acceptable and feasible. Stanford was not going to be happy as that was often how he would pay for things such as lunch out, dinner for friends, or new things for Julia to enjoy. Well, hell, he would just have to learn to cope. That was the only method in which Stanford and Julia were going to be able to keep the home!

If they didn't have the home, then where would the kids come back to? Where would they have their memories? How could they hold their heads up and look their friends in the eye? Stop that! Positive thoughts only! How did we get to this point! Stop it! Right now! Her thoughts were swirling rapidly as she tried to find a way to get back to the spot of positive thoughts.

Positive thoughts included the next strategy. After credit card negotiations, she would need to speak to the mortgage company about the best method to salvage her family home. Yet, she doubted that her kids were near as attached to it as she was. It was important to her…she had big plans… they just weren't easy to complete as her ideas were often grandiose and came second to either the kids' or Stanford's' desires. Maybe it was time to put her priorities first.

That would mean setting a strict budget in which she herself had little interest other than the actual outcome-her future. Okay, let's get started.

She had spoken with the credit card companies. They weren't happy with her plan. They wanted much more than she was willing to give. That was too bad. She couldn't continue to give what they wanted. That was accomplished.

The mortgage company was even less thrilled with her proposal. However, she was able to paint a future picture that did give some improved outlook. They were willing to work on that premise plus the fact that if it didn't work out, they would be at a much better place to sell at a larger profit as the economy improved.

Okay, that only left both herself and Stanford to buy into the restrictions. That meant that there would be very little money to go out, even for a drink. Not for a while unless things dramatically changed for their businesses. They would still have their home. They would still have their vehicles. They would still be able to work. They would have trouble looking friends in the eye. But they would be able to live.

She felt good! Finally!

CHAPTER 2

That was the last thought as she went to sleep. She never knew what happened.

Stanford had been plotting for some time. He had set the gas timer for 6am. He was out of the house on his way for his first passenger to be picked up. He was able to act extremely surprised when the call came over the radio for him to come to the bus yard when finished with the morning run. He was expecting it. Yet, wasn't it funny that you would radio ahead to inform him to do what he was expecting to do like any other day on the job.

He finished dropping the last passenger at school. He took the bus to the bus yard. Waiting on him there was the sheriff. He said he was sorry to inform him that there had been a terrible accident at the house. It had exploded. They were still trying to get all of the fires contained to see what damage had been done, who had gotten hurt, how it had started. Was there anything that they could do for him? Stanford was having great difficulty containing himself.

"How?" "When?" "Where's Julia?" "The kids?"

"Oh my God!" as he wails and thrashes around as if in disbelief and fear. All the while, experiencing a feeling of elation and revelation. He was free. Finally free. No more Julia. No more kids. He could rid himself of the property. Pay off all the debts. Start over. He could finally pursue that beautiful young attorney that had recently moved into their circle of friends. Of course, he would need to wait a little while before starting that relationship. He could accept her condolences or any assistance that she was willing to give while waiting.

Wow! This was what freedom felt like!

The sheriff was saying something. He should be paying attention! What if it was important? "Once the fire is put out, we will be able to determine what the cause was. Once that it is determined, we can let you see what you can salvage from there."

Did he prepare it well enough to prevent any suggestions of arson? Did he have all of his bases covered? Had he went far enough away to purchase the pipe cutter? Was there any way to check on the timer?

Too late to think of these things. It was important for him to act like a worried husband and father. What was that the sheriff was saying?

"Looks like the neighbors were already at work and didn't get hurt."

Oh my goodness. He hadn't even considered how it would impact the neighbors. How was he going to deal with that? Don't think of that, he wasn't supposed to know anything. So…he just sat there with his head in his hands… waiting for time to pass and things to move forward. Then

Ralph said it was not a good idea for him to drive his afternoon route. Now what was he to do? No home to go home to. No family to go to the hotel with. Maybe he should see if one of his friends would let him room for the night.

Where was his cell phone? He could call Jessie to see if he was willing to give him a place to stay at least for tonight.

Okay, Jessie was agreeable. That was until Janice came home tomorrow. Then it might be another story altogether. Okay, one day at a time. The sheriff said it was okay to go to Jessie's but to stay in touch so that if they needed anything else, they could contact him.

It was hard not to speed as he was driving along. It was even harder to convince the sheriff and Ralph that he didn't need a ride to Jessie's house. But, he had been able to convince them he was okay to drive that short 15 minute drive to Jessie's house.

He began to sing:

"Julia, Julia, my dearest Julia, oh how you light up my life.
You give me hope that there is still a chance to be happy!
I will miss you Julia, Julia, no longer my wife!
It will be a chore to tell your pappy! (He couldn't stop laughing)

It's too bad that you went up in smoke after the big bang!
Julia, Julia, now there is no more strife!
This is much more effective than to hang!
Julia, Julia, you light up my life!

Oh Julia, Julia, I get to start all over again
Without you hanging on to my chin
No more Julia, Julia to stop my fun
I will once more get to have fun with my run!"

Wow! He just made that up on the spur of the moment. He should have taped it so that he could use it when he was feeling down and needed a pick me up. Oh well, he would just have to try and remember it or improvise as he went along.

Okay, at Jessie's. He was being overprotective and overbearing. How was he to get rid of him? He would lay down for a nap. That was effective.

Now, he needed to think about his plan. He had managed to carry out the initial part. Yet, he needed to stick to his story to keep things working the way they needed to. He had told the sheriff, Ralph, and Jessie the same story.

He had awakened at the same time he always does, did what he always does, and came to work not noticing anything different or unusual as he did so. That was his story and he was sticking with it. It would keep him out of trouble. He wouldn't be recognized by anyone at the hardware store where he had purchased the pipe cutter or the timer.

CHAPTER 3

Meanwhile at the scene of his home, the entire neighborhood was upset. Not only did it appear that his family was annihilated, the next door neighbors had lost their home, favorite pet, and the antique car. Where was Stanford? Didn't he care what had happened? You would think he would have tried to come to see if they could find anything that was important to him. The neighbors were having great difficulty understanding his ability to stay away as requested by the sheriff.

The sheriff was busy checking the area for any suspicious characters, what might have been a motive for the arson that he had not told anyone he suspected. He was also looking into the Shotts' finances to see if there might have been a financial motive to have caused the fire. There was definitely a need to have some fast cash in their hands. The Shotts were in desperate financial straits. They owed all of their credit cards. They were almost losing their house to foreclosure. They didn't have many options for recouping their losses without something drastic like this. In addition, the first firefighter at the scene stated he had not seen any bodies in the wreckage. This was something he didn't want to get out as he wasn't sure if this would be an important piece of the investigation or not.

The firefighter was initially reluctant to keep his mouth shut, but then had understood that if it was arson, the family may be in danger or the cause of the blast in the first place. It was only then that the firefighter agreed to keep his mouth shut. Next, the sheriff needed to speak with the arson investigator to confirm or deny it was arson. Thus, he was quite happy that Stanford didn't have the wherewithal to understand that he should have come to the fire site.

The arson investigator was also reluctant to keep quiet about the fact that it was definitely arson. He would need to carry out his investigation somewhat secretively without the neighborhood finding out that there was indeed an arsonist on the loose that could put them next in the line of a blast. Yet, the arson investigator would do it quietly so as to not let anyone know that it was actually a known arson.

The sheriff was beginning to get a good feel for the process occurring. The Shotts were having a horrendous time trying to make ends meet. Then they found that there were only a couple of ways to accomplish their escape from their financial burdens. The first was just letting things go back to the banks. The next had been to file for bankruptcy. Another was the lottery-like that was going to help. Another had been to attempt the short sale suggested by the bank that Stanford had refused to do. Last, but not least, was to collect the insurance money from life and property insurance -

apparently the most attractive. This was the option that was chosen, at least, by Stanford.

The sheriff's job now was to put the nails into the coffin cementing Stanford's journey to the jailhouse. The arson investigator stated there was a timer used to let the gas escape through the tiny holes created by the pipe cutters which ignited from a pilot light. It would take some time to sift through all of the rubble to find out if any of those items were amongst Stanford's tools.

Since Stanford had taken his advice and went to a friend's house, he had plenty of time to sift through the rubble. Unfortunately, that was not as easy to do as he might want it to be. The rubble was varying in consistency, height, location. How was he to determine what was was originally in the shed outside? What might have been in the house? Well, the arson investigator, Stanley, was able to pinpoint that there was no accelerant applied anywhere or any trail from one. He had also said there was a probable initial spark from the oven pilot light, but more likely from the hot water heater. If that were the case, then what had created the explosion?

Well, what was next to a pilot light? Natural gas of course! What was the condition of the lines? Any deliberate cuts? Normal wear and tear of the lines? How was he to determine that? Where was Stanley when he needed him most? Stanley's expertise would prove useful for that determination.

Why weren't Julia and the kids present? Were they part of the crime or just lucky to have left prior to the explosion? Did he really want to exclude this information from Stanford? It seemed best to keep it quiet until determining if they were involved or innocent.

Next step was to exercise the option of arson investigator or have Stanley come back to the scene to perform the arson investigation.

"Stanley, sorry to do this on a holiday weekend and all, but could you expedite the investigative portion of the fire beginnings? It would really help to expedite the process and then you could possibly be entirely honest a little earlier if we were able to finish the process."

"Carl, it just isn't possible right this minute. I will need to gather all of the necessary people to wrap it up. I just gave them all the three day weekend off. Most are already 90 minutes away. You will just have to make do for the weekend as it will be 7 am on Monday when we start back up."

"Oh come on, Stanley, work with me."

"I made it quite clear when we started the process it was now or not until next week. You stated you weren't sure how fast you wanted to move on it. I made an executive decision to cut administrative costs by letting the guys go for a long weekend that was long overdue. Suck it up!" Then Stanley hung up and wouldn't answer as Carl kept trying to redial.

Well, that made it necessary to get an idea now. Okay, time to start looking at the rubble for possible parts to create a timer or other device to ignite the fire. Since the fire seemed to have started either at the oven or hot water heater, that was the most likely place to start looking. According to the plans for the home, that would be in the most northwestern corner of the property or central southern portion. Carl decided to take the most likely as well as easiest area to access – the northwestern corner.

He initially took some photos from multiple angles so as to be able to recreate any necessary recreations for Stanley as necessary. Now, he slowly shifted the rubble to the west inch by inch looking for any wiring, trigger devices, cogwheels, frayed wiring, or other suspicious items. Nothing so far and he had been looking for the last hour. He had only moved four inches of rubble. This was going to take forever. If he didn't do this now though, he risked letting Stanford come back to the site and remove any incriminating evidence. That would be a crying shame. Yet, it wouldn't hurt if he took a short break to eat something and then come back to the site to look some more.

He again took multiple photos from different angles to keep track of the progress as well as anything that may be out of place upon his return. He then left to go to the local bar for some much needed refreshments. He ordered a simple hamburger, fries, and a large ice tea when he really wanted some nuts and a tall beer. While waiting on the order, he reviewed the details that he had so far.

CHAPTER 4

$\sim\sim\sim\sim\sim\sim\sim\sim\sim\sim\sim\sim\sim\sim\sim$

First, there was a large explosion at 6:05 am this morning that rocked the neighborhood. Immediately after the explosion, the phone lines were lit up at 911 announcing the explosion at 74-5207 Thompson Drive. The 911 operator activated all services immediately including the police, fire, and ambulance personnel. First on the scene were the neighbors who simply monitored the progress. Next, were the firefighters, Greg Chowdry and Terry Sample. They stated they immediately assessed the situation, proceeded to remove their hoses, and suit up to check the insides of the two homes for any damages as well as any potential victims that might need saving. That took them mere minutes and then they were progressing into the house when he and the policemen, Douglas Fairbanks and Crabby Firepit, arrived. They formed a perimeter around the property encouraging the growing crowd to write down their impressions, their names, addresses, and phone numbers for future reference upon the circulating clipboard. The ambulance crew arrived just as Greg and Terry were exiting the building. They announced there wasn't anyone left in the buildings. That was when Carl had simply stated that information was to remain confidential. No one seemed happy about that little piece, but none had voiced their objections. Since it was technically outside of city limits, the police were quite happy to relinquish control to Carl. They continued to assist with crowd control while Greg and Terry brought the flames under control. Once that was accomplished, Carl had ascertained that Stanford had left early for work driving the school bus and would be shortly coming back to the bus yard. It was at that time that he had left to speak to Stanford Shotts about the fire and to inform him that there didn't appear to be any survivors as well as completely demolishing the neighbor's property as well. Stanford didn't seem initially to respond but then had been almost overdramatic like he had rehearsed his response. Then, when he stated he could drive to a friend's house by himself and had done so quite safely and calmly according to the intermittent eye in the sky report Carl had received, it supported even more of a arson and attempted murder if that was indeed what he had intended to happen. Stanford had stayed at the friend's house, Jessie, and hadn't left as of yet, even to check out the fire, the damage, anything that he may salvage. Apparently, he was unaware that a truly caring husband and father would be looking for any potential clues as well as what he could salvage of that relationship. Stanford was not. That was going to be his undoing. The neighbors were also going to crucify him if what they were commenting on upon Carl's return to the scene was any indication. They thought he was a coldhearted bastard for not returning to see what, if anything, he could do, who had been hurt, if anything had been left that he could keep. Then when Carl had been sifting through the rubble, there hadn't been any evidence so far. However, he would return as soon as he finished with his food which had just arrived.

After eating all that food, Carl felt like he could just go to sleep. He should have chosen the veggie plate. Oh well, he would just have to work on his full stomach to find those clues. Wait; stop at the corner Piggly Wiggly to get a couple of diet sodas to assist with the thirst and monotony of this investigation.

That was an interesting stop as well. Everyone at the Piggly Wiggly was discussing the fire and explosion and sharing their opinions of the family, the situation in which they had found themselves, as well as what they thought had actually happened according to which family member they knew as well as what they had witnessed in the preceding weeks. One fellow, Josh, stated he had worked with Stanford for many years and that he was a hard fellow to get to know. He thought that made it difficult to ascertain what Stanford may or may not have done. He was also unaware of any money problems. That was not the case of Sally, the cashier. She knew Stanford much better as he tended to come in every morning to get a coffee on the way to the bus yard. She had noticed quite evidently he had not done so this morning. When he bought his morning coffees, he would always have a quick comment about how it was getting harder and harder to even buy the coffee. He had started saving all of his lose change just to be able to afford the purchase of his morning coffees. He also seemed to blame his wife, Julia, for all of the bad luck that they were having. Always complaining about how lazy she was, how she never seemed to know how to make the dime stretch farther like his own good mother had been good at, how she had gained weight over the years and wasn't able to fit into many of her clothes as of late. Sally thought that he was unhappy, poor, and vindictive.

She had stated she didn't doubt that he had set the fire.

Justin, another customer, didn't think he had enough gumption or capability to have even planned it. Justin's opinion was that Stanford was just too lazy and stupid to have even been able to have started the process, let alone complete it. He did, however, think that Stanford may have been too lazy to have made the necessary repairs to prevent a potential hazard such as a broken gas line or frayed electrical cords.

Anastacia, another customer, stated she had just had coffee with Julia the other day. Julia was frantic trying to find different fast ways to make enough money to keep the home, let alone, her family intact. Julia had also insinuated that Stanford might have been a little abusive. Anastacia had left that morning concerned about her friend's wellbeing, her overall safety, and whether or not Stanford indeed might be that abusive to try something. Then the explosion and fire where he was the only one left standing made her quite suspicious.

Harry, another neighbor, found the Shotts to be quite a reclusive family avoiding any exposure to the limelight. He said the kids often would be seen just outside the door but never far away from the house other than to go to school. If you happened to say hello to one of them, they practically run back into the house and you wouldn't see them come out for days. He had found that strange, but couldn't put his finger on anything that would lead to an actual investigation or prevention of this outcome. They had always managed to stay just that little bit under the radar.

More fodder to add to his investigation so far. Carl proceeded back to the scene more energized after listening to the conversation at the Piggly Wiggly.

Where did he leave off? Oh, here's the spot. Inch by inch he moved the debris little by little so as to not miss any potential evidence. He had been at this for more than four hours without even a small piece of any evidence being found. He had managed to clear simply a foot of area. Time to take another picture to compare and remember what objects had been where. Take a little break and drink some of the diet soda. He was unsure how long he had dozed, but the sun was far down in the sky. He didn't have much light left to look over the evidence. He checked his cell phone, no missed calls. Obviously, he wasn't going to get any help before the first of the following week. He decided to ask for the security to maintain the patency of the scene while he went to get a tent and some flood lights to enable him to keep at this through the weekend. He would also have all of the time in the world to sift through his thoughts organizing what he learned as he went.

CHAPTER 5

After pitching the tent and placing the flood lights in such a manner as to not disturb as many neighbors as he could, he proceeded to continue to dig through the rubble for any pieces of wiring, any areas that might show the trail of the explosion. He worked long into the night without any interference. It was almost midnight when he realized that he hadn't eaten his evening meal. He was not going to eat it either as he was dog tired. He was going to sleep. He took his final pictures for the day then turned out the flood lights. He was exhausted so went right to sleep.

When he awoke, he had trouble orienting himself as to where he was, what he had been doing. Then it hit him, he had spent the night at the explosion site sifting through rubble looking for clues. There was barely any light outside, but something had awakened him. There it was again. That scraping noise. What was that? He tried to remain calm while he searched quietly for his pants so that he could investigate what the noise was. He hurriedly donned his pants and then peeked from inside of the tent. There at the rubble site was Stanford, sifting through the rubble using a flashlight. Stanford was so intent upon his purpose; he hadn't noticed Carl poking his head from behind the tent flap. That explained the reason why it didn't seem like it was light outside yet as well as the scraping noise. However, it didn't explain why Stanford was sifting through the rubble. Instead of confronting him, Carl decided to watch as well as snapping some pictures without Stanford's knowledge. The pictures might come in handy later when trying to prove that Stanford had been looking for some incriminating evidence.

Whoops! Stanford saw him taking pictures. You would have thought Stanford would have taken off running. Instead, he continued doing what he was doing. Well, maybe he would just continue doing the watching and filming while letting Stanford lead him to the evidence instead of sifting through it for himself. That might be the best solution. Yet, Carl couldn't understand why Stanford would allow himself to be watched and photographed while sifting through the rubble. Finally after watching and filming Stanford for another two hours, Carl couldn't contain his curiosity anymore. He went over to where Stanford was sifting through the rubble to ask him what he was looking for.

Stanford turned to look at him as he approached. "What's wrong? It's my house isn't it? That makes this my rubble."

"I was wondering what you were actually looking for. Did you forget something this morning before going to work?"

"I was looking for something that I left in the shed a couple of days ago and can't find it." Stanford replied.

"Would you like some assistance? It might go faster if two of us were looking instead of just one of us." Carl responded to see what Stanford would say.

"I don't need your help." Stanford replied.

"Well….since we haven't cleared this for you to come in and look for things, I could arrest you for breaking and entering. Didn't you see the yellow crime scene tape when you entered the property?"

"I thought that was to keep all of the riffraff from stealing anything that may have survived the explosion, not ME!" Stanford replied.

"It's time for you to leave or I will be forced to arrest you for trespassing on your own property since it is actually a crime scene until cleared. Or you could simply tell me what you were looking for and we might be able to solve this right now as I had already cleared a good portion of the area where you are looking hours ago."

"If you didn't want me on the property looking for something, why did you allow me to do so without arresting me?"

Carl replied, "I thought you may find what you were looking for or at the very least feel guilty about looking when you sensed that I was watching and taking photos. Then I realized that you hadn't found what you were looking for and that you might be looking for a particular memento. That doesn't seem to be the case either, as you are still searching and will not share what you are looking for. Therefore, it seems that you may be guilty of a crime. As such, I can't continue to let you look for something that may be a piece of critical evidence. So either you leave peacefully or I will have to put you under arrest. That's the least that I can do for someone who has just lost his family, home, and doesn't know what he is looking for at … (looks at his watch) four am."

Stanford just looked at Carl incredulously during the entire statement. It was then that he broke down and started sobbing. "I can't find the Buick or the keys."

Now it was Carl's opportunity to look at Stanford incredulously. "Buick?"

"Yes. It was Julia's car. My old clunker has quite a bit of trouble getting around so I thought that if I could find the keys to the car, I could drive it around instead of my old clunker."

Well that a plausible solution to what he was looking for. Yet, it still didn't make sense why he would easily assume the Buick would still be there when it was just a pile of rubble. He couldn't possibly think that the Buick would be in functioning condition even if it were beneath the rubble that had been the garage. The best solution would be to placate Stanford with the promise that once the scene was released the Buick would be returned to him if they found it or the keys. With the promise that the Buick would be returned, Stanford had simply turned and left without another word.

CHAPTER 6

Carl, however, was wide awake. He continued where Stanford had left off after taking pictures of the site prior to restarting the process. He was able to see in the predawn well enough to know if what he was seeing was part of evidence or just normal explosive fire rubble and ashes. After spending the next four hours sifting through the rubble, he felt ravenous. It was then that he realized that he hadn't eaten since yesterday evening. It was time to take pictures again and fix himself something to eat.

Carl had been clearing the rubble for the last two days without any evidence being unearthed. Today, he could turn that over to Stanley and his staff. That would free Carl up to look for additional information to support an attempted murder as well as arson or insurance fraud and arson. First thing he was going to do was to eat a real meal instead of the sandwich style meats he had had all weekend.

After completing his meal, he proceeded to the computer at the office to look at what he had compiled thus far. He inputted all of the information that he had compiled as of yet. Once he had done that, he looked up information on Stanford, Julia, the kids, their extended family, past work experiences, current experiences, and where they had lived previously. This was more time consuming than his sifting through the rubble at the crime scene. He took a break after six hours to eat another meal and to take a walk to encourage his brain to function more efficiently. After coming back from his walk, he looked at the information he had compiled from his internet searches thus far.

Stanford had been born March 24, 1967 in a small town in Maryland to parents, Jasper and Christina Shotts. He had a rather unremarkable childhood as there were no records of any arrests, school problems, or complaints either against Stanford or his parents. He graduated high school and proceeded to go to the local college, Frostburg State University. Once again, nothing unusual noted during his college years. He graduated with his degree in anthropology and moved to Phoenix, Arizona, to be closer to multiple anthropological digs. During his first year there, he had met Julia, a local nursing student. They had begun to date while she had attended nursing school. They married after she graduated and she continued to support the two of them on her salary as a nurse at Mayo Clinic. She delivered their first child, a son they named Jasper, three years later. By this time, Julia had begun to notice that their funds were entirely dependent upon her and that Stanford had never worked. There was a temporary separation at that time. They reconciled after Stanford started working at a local 7-11 store. There were no other highlights noted in his search other than the birth of their daughter, Catherine, three years after Jasper's birth. The children had attended first the Head Start program, then the elementary school nearby. It was only when the economy started to turn downwards, that there seemed to be more obvious problems rearing their ugly heads. First, Jasper had been having trouble at school. There were multiple notations of the parents being asked to come and talk with the principal. It was also noted that only Julia had come to those meetings explaining that there were some difficulties at home which she never elaborated upon. Too bad no one had picked up on this silent clue that there was something occurring. Just one more missed opportunity to have salvaged the entire explosion and possible murder. This made it look coincidental that Julia and the kids were not at the home when it exploded. It was beginning to look like an abused family had escaped a bad situation at the right time.

Whoops! He was getting off of the objective phase of his investigation. Carl proceeded to look at the rest of the downloaded information. Julia had quit her job approximately nine months previously further reducing their income. The Mayo Clinic insinuated there was a slight problem with her having to leave too much to be at home with her kids during illnesses, etc., and had been encouraged to take an early retirement with the benefits to not start until she was 60. Since she was the major breadwinner, which was a huge impact upon their available spending habits. Yet, it didn't seem to impact the way in which Stanford had use his credit cards or his spending habits. The credit report noted the beginning of problems approximately six months earlier. At this time there was a decline in both Jasper's and Catherine's grade from the A's that they had been getting to C's and D's. It was another potential sign that could have prevented this disaster from occurring if someone had been paying closer attention and had reacted. Well, it hadn't been obvious to those involved and now was a missed opportunity. It seemed to Carl that their needed to be a better understanding of things that often lead to a disaster if not diverted at an early enough date. After this investigation, he might just have to work towards a process to prevent this disaster from recurring by increasing community awareness of the potential warning signs that had been overlooked and what could have been more effectively evaluated prior to something of this caliber occurring.

Getting back to the subject at hand, there had been a fight at the last party Stanford and Julia had attended. It had caused his office to respond, but no arrests had been filed. Julia had refused to acknowledge that Stanford had hit her in plain view of the other guests or that he might do so again. The abused spouse rarely does. His own office could have possibly prevented this when questioning the other guests that attended. If any had been willing to file the complaint, it would not have mattered if Julia would not. Stanford had seemed regretful to his officer so he had not pursued the further investigation of other guests. When looking at the list of guests, he happened to notice one of the community's newest residents was one of the attendees. She was the newest addition to the Landers Law Firm. He wondered why she hadn't proceeded forward with any complaints. However, he hadn't noticed her amongst many of the gatherings in the community. Maybe, after that fiasco two months ago, she was reluctant to attend any other social gatherings. Actually, upon further review of these notes, maybe he should visit with Blair Underwood, the new lawyer, before moving forward.

With that thought in mind, he proceeded to the law offices of Landers Law Firm. They should be close to closing time making his visit less of an impact upon Ms. Underwood's practice. Ms. Underwood had known it was only a matter of time before someone had come to see her about her interpretation of the party's fiasco after hearing about the explosion on the news. She was reluctant to speak to anyone as of yet, but Carl, the local sheriff didn't seem to be near as slow at putting two and two together as she had anticipated.

She welcomed the sheriff and offered him a cup of coffee. "What can I do for you officer?"

"Black would be nice. I have a few questions regarding Mr. and Mrs. Shotts, especially at a party that you attended a couple of months ago." Carl responded.

"What exactly would you like to know?" Blair hedged.

"Were you present during the party where the Shotts had an argument and skirmish?"

"Yes."

"Did you witness the skirmish?"

"Yes."

"Do you have to be a typical lawyer and answer only in minimal answers? I thought that you would at least be willing to provide some insight into the situation between the two of them from someone who knew neither one very well and possibly maintain that objectivity. Explain your interpretation of the skirmish as well as the preceding events and anything you witnessed after the skirmish. Please." Carl pleaded with Blair.

"I am sorry but unfortunately I am unable to satisfy your curiosity. I must maintain client confidentiality."

"What are you talking about?"

"Stanford Shotts proceeded to our offices this morning after you kicked him off of his property this weekend. He was waiting at the door when we opened. He insisted upon me helping him with the potential for a case being built against him. Even if he hadn't insisted upon me being his legal counsel, I am the junior associate and would have been assigned his case." Blair responded.

"What the_ _ _ _?" Carl ranted and then simply gave in to his frustration and groaned extremely loud, loud enough to make Blair uncomfortable. He took a deep cleansing breath before asking his next question. "What do you feel comfortable sharing with me that doesn't interfere with your client confidentiality?"

"I'm sorry, but there isn't anything that I can directly share with you. I could suggest that you speak with Abner Cransbert, Cory Cransbert, Harry Wiseman, and Larry Picks. They were immediately adjacent to the skirmish as you describe it and might be willing to give you their interpretations of that episode." Blair attempted to lighten her inability to assist in the investigation.

"One last question. Why didn't you come forward when Julia refused to file charges against Stanford at that time?"

"I was reluctant to get involved as I was not familiar with all of the players, nor how I would be accepted if I had done so just moving into the community. Where I come from, if the victim refuses to press charges, there is nothing that can be done to keep the perpetrator from continuing to do it over and over again. It was only after the episode that I researched and found out that I could have filed the charges also. Looking back, I wished that I had done so. Hindsight being 20/20 and all."

Carl thanked her for her honesty and left frustrated. It was time to get to Abner and Cory Cransbert and get their interpretation of the skirmish. That would probably prove to be a waste of time as Cory also was an abused spouse who bore the marks beneath her clothing. Abner was an abusive spouse who had learned to keep evidence out of the view of others including the skirmishes, arguments, and visual proof of such. He would probably prove to be protective of Stanford while Cory would keep her mouth as shut as Abner required.

CHAPTER 7

Carl was right. Abner had denied there was even a disagreement at the party. He denied any physical interaction between Stanford and Julia other than the dancing and the tripping that had led up to the teasing about her clumsiness. Cory had agreed with Abner's version with nods never once saying a single word. Of course, that was not the least bit surprising. You would think she would come forward fearing for her own life as everyone had assumed that Julia and the kids had expired in the fire. But, it was not to be so.

He left their home and proceeded to Harry Wiseman's home. It was getting close to supper time and he should be at home waiting on his wife to make their evening meal. Harry was also reluctant to share any information. He had been noncommittal, denying any actual skirmish occurring.

What was going on? Carl could understand the Cransbert's denial, but what was Harry's problem with relating what had occurred? He would have to look at any connections to Stanford and Julia.

CHAPTER 8

Carl left to eat and then went home to get a good night's sleep so that he could tackle this with a fresh mind and new view on the situation. When he arose in the morning, he felt refreshed. He was ready to research some more, especially before interviewing Larry Picks. He didn't want to be unaware of any contacts, friendships, past interactions, as well as past discrepancies / indiscretions that he might be able to use for leverage in his interviews.

After three hours of internet research, he looked at the individuals, the churches they attended, the different civic groups in which they were members, what restaurants they went to, who was friends with whom, and whether any were known associates with any of the others. Despite this research, he was unable to find any ties between the players with which he would be interviewing. That meant he still didn't understand why Harry was so uncooperative. Maybe, after talking with Larry, he would go back and see Harry again and try to jog his memory. Ten minutes later he was at Larry's work place. Larry was just opening the doors as Carl pulled up to the doorway. He looked at Carl with a questioning glance.

"What's up, Carl?"

"I have a few questions to try and sort out this explosion business. Do you have a few minutes to help me process the Shotts' relationship?"

"I'm just opening up. As long as no customers come in, I have a few minutes." Larry responded.

"Do you remember the party 2 months ago when Stanford and Julia were in a heated discussion and he struck her?"

"That's not exactly how I remember it. They were getting more animated when Julia tried to pull out of his grasp. It appeared that Stanford pulled her back so fast that she ran into his hand as sort of a normal retraction jerk as she swung back into his arms." Larry responded.

"Does that mean he didn't strike her? That it was an accident? Did you ever see them fighting before that? Did he have anger issues with the kids?" Carl asked steadily getting louder as he asked the questions.

"Whoa! Back up just a minute, Carl. Stanford actually was a good father, spent time with the kids during the activities that they did attend. He didn't fight with Julia any more than any other married couple on the block. There was never a need to call the cops because it seemed to get out of control."

Carl decided that he wasn't going to get any more than that so he thanked Larry for his time and left. He quickly went over to Harry's to ask him if he remembered any more details.

Carl left Harry's just as frustrated as when he left Larry's. Now what was he supposed to do? It was time to regroup and think of what his goal was, who he needed to interview, what if any evidence he might need / have.

CHAPTER 9

Going back over the details was most important. There was an explosion at 6:30 am on Friday morning. The fire department arrived first with no victims found and then they proceeded to put out the resultant fires. It destroyed both the Schotts' home as well as the neighbor's home.

When Stanford Schotts was notified of the explosion and fire, he assumed that his wife and kids were killed and hadn't insisted upon returning to the scene to try and find any of them, went docilely to a friend's house. Then he had returned in the middle of the night to his home site supposedly to look for car keys and the car. He stated it was because his car didn't run too well. He left the crime scene none too happily and sought the assistance of an attorney.

This attorney was one of those at the party two months prior who had seen him strike his spouse during a heated discussion preventing her from even discussing her perceptions of the discussion. His resultant discussions with potential witnesses also seemed to recall it differently than what was initially described to him.

In addition, the neighborhood Piggly Wiggly customers had expressed concerning opinions, most pointing to a not so rosy relationship between Stanford and Julia. The review of their pasts was mostly unremarkable other than the older child, Jasper, acting out behavior, both kids' recent grades declining, and the Schotts' recent decline in their finances.

Couple these facts together; it still seemed that the explosion was not accidental, but purposeful. The additional question was whether it also included insurance fraud with Julia involved or attempted murder of Julia and the kids.

So, given these facts, he should probably see if he might find Julia and the kids.

CHAPTER 10

Where were Julia and the kids? Where might they have gone if they didn't want Stanford to know where to find them? How could they disappear without anyone knowing they had gone?

Of course! Women's shelters were infamous for bringing in the women and families of abused families in such a manner as to prevent the abuser from knowing where to find them. They had learned it was to their advantage to keep the authorities from knowing these facts. That would explain why he had not been able to find them easily.

He made one phone call to the abuse hotline. He explained that he was the local sheriff, he was looking for Julia Schotts and the kids, that he only needed to speak to them over the phone to ask them some questions about the explosion, and if need be to have them testify at a later date in the trial. The woman on the other end of the phone stated she would relay the information to individual shelters to see if she and the kids were at one of the sites, she would have the opportunity to call back on a secure phone line. Now, all he had to do was wait to see if his bait would get a return phone call.

CHAPTER 11

Stanford was scared. He had moved out of Jessie's house yesterday after his wife, Janice, had come home. He had moved into a cheap motel in a not so good part of town. Then when he had gone out to the truck this morning, all four tires were slit. It was going to seem funny completing a police report about this, but it would have to be done. The frightening thing was that he needed the insurance money from the explosion and Julia and the kids deaths to be able to move to a safer area. That would have to wait.

He picked up the phone and called the police. After completing the report, he called Ralph to see if he could come pick him up for work. Ralph told him to wait until next week to come back to work. Ralph said he would cover the shifts until then.

Next, he called the Allstate insurance company to file a claim for the tires. They said it would be three days before he would be able to pick up the check. It would cover the cost of cheap tires, not the ones that he had had on the truck. Once again, where were the Buick and the keys to the Buick? Where was Carl's phone number to ask him about that?

CHAPTER 12

Upon his arrival at the office this morning, Carl was surprised to find a report for four slit tires on Stanford's truck sitting on his desk as well as a request from Stanford asking about the Buick. It also listed his temporary address in a not so nice part of town. No wonder the tires had been slit. His truck was a beacon for vandalism in that part of town.

Carl decided to call Stanley to find out what he had discerned from the remains at the explosion site. Stanley confirmed he had found pieces of what looked like a timer. He was in the process of trying to find where it had been bought, who might have built the piece, or given instruction on its construction. He was also certain that there was no possible victims, no Buick, as well as informing the insurance company that it was indeed arson-without a confirmed arsonist as of yet. He had let the insurance company know to not let Stanford know he might be on the list of suspects until proven innocent and to stall about any payments.

Carl proceeded to the bus yard to talk with Stanford. When he arrived, Ralph asked what he was doing there as Stanford was not due back at work until next week. Since he was unable to talk with Stanford, he decided to get a feel for what Ralph thought of Stanford, the Schotts, and their relationship, whether there were any problems or concerns that Stanford had shared. When Carl was done speaking with Ralph, he didn't know any more than when he came in other than Stanford was a very punctual, dependable employee that Ralph wanted to keep.

Carl decided to put together a mapping of the entire crime and see if he could come up with any additional thoughts or ideas regarding the direction that he should pursue or questions to ask. That took him approximately four hours to arrange the different pieces of the crime in such a way that they made sense to him.

Candi, his telephone operator, took one look at the mapping board and asked, "Where are Julia and the kids?"

Carl responded, "I'm not sure. They weren't any bodies. There was no evidence of the family car in the rubble. No one has reported her missing, no one has called stating that she was her, and there just haven't been any clues. I called the shelters asking if they knew her, if they had been contacted by her, they would call or at least have her call. But, I haven't heard anything from that direction either. Any ideas?"

Candi just shook her head.

Then the unexpected happened. Stanford walked in. "Have you found my Buick yet? What is going on with the investigation? Have you cleared the potential for arson? How do I go about getting the death certificates for Julia and the kids? Why hasn't the coroner contacted me to identify something of theirs? Them? Why haven't you said something? Are you going to give me any answers? Well?"

Carl had halted the demands with a hand up stop sign like movement. Stanford had finally stopped demanding an answer and stopped talking long enough for Carl to respond. "First, I had just had confirmation from Stanley, the fire investigator, that it is indeed arson. That makes it a little more drawn out as it is now an investigation of who might have set the fire. He also mentioned he could not say if there were any bodies to identify as he didn't actually find any. Nor did he find any cars. However, the explosion and fire were quite dramatic and hot and could have devoured any evidence of such….which means that the hint of arson will delay any insurance payouts until the investigation is complete."

"What are you talking about? How am I going to get around? Someone slit all four of my truck tires. It was already on its last leg. I told you that the other day when you asked me what I was looking for. I really need the Buick to get around. Now you are telling me that I can't even access the insurance payments to get some money to buy some new tires, a new vehicle, anything!"

Carl allowed him the privilege of venting as anyone would be frustrated when facing very little if no options. Then Carl reminded Stanford that he had a lawyer through whom he should communicate so that no improprieties were violated or relinquish her services. With that reminder, Stanford proceeded to stomp out. Carl hoped it was to bother Blair as she had used the client confidentiality law to her benefit and he had just used the "you have a lawyer and I can't talk to you without the lawyer present" line. At least that had felt good.

Candi asked why he had shared the information that he had and why he hadn't covered the board. Carl wondered if Stanford had even noticed the board or what was on it. He would have to put it in his office facing the wall so that it was not easily visible from the doorway or the window to protect his thoughts. But, first, he needed to add Stanford's frustration with the lack of money and his four slit tires.

CHAPTER 13

Stanford did proceed right over to Blair's office walking in as if he owned the place. He strode right into her office while she was in the middle of interviewing another client about his upcoming court case. She stood up with an angry look on her face and walked around her desk, grabbed Stanford's arm, walked him out to the waiting room, and told her secretary to schedule him an appointment. She walked back into her office and locked the door.

She proceeded to speak once again with her client when Stanford began pounding on the door. She didn't even flinch when she picked up the phone, dialed 911, and placed a complaint about a violent person pounding unwanted on her door. She then placed another call to her employer and announced that she would be firing the client pounding on her door for aggressive behavior. After completing these phone calls, she inquired of her current client if he would like to continue now or at a later time. They left the office running. She doubted she would be trying that case after all.

Upon seeing the door opening and the client rushing out, Stanford attempted to enter her office when she managed just barely to close the door firmly before he did so. Then she heard the sirens. She was thankful that Stanford didn't have a clue they were for him. He was surprised when the police came in looking for the suspect and the secretary pointed at him. They rushed him and had him in handcuffs asking him if he understood his rights. What rights? He wasn't even aware of what they had been telling him while cuffing him. Exactly what had he done? Would someone please explain it to him?

After the police had arrested Stanford, Blair called up Carl asking for a meeting at a local dining facility. She met him there at 5:30 for drinks and appetizers.

Carl arrived late purposefully since Blair had been unhelpful before. "What's up?"

Blair looked at Carl disdainfully. Apparently he was unaware of what she had instigated earlier today. "I thought it might be a good idea to discuss the party events that you were interested in earlier since I no longer represent Stanford after filing charges earlier against him."

Carl looked at her quizzically. He was unsure of what she was talking about. So, instead of asking her about the party, he asked, "What charges?"

She explained what occurred in the office. Then she started laughing as she explained what the video camera in her reception area had caught on Stanford's face was such a look of disbelief as the officers had cuffed him.

Carl apologized for instigating that situation. He explained that he had just told Stanford that it was going to be some time before he could obtain any insurance monies as they thought it might be a case of arson and that was as much as he could tell him as he should only be speaking to Stanford's attorney.

Blair looked at Carl incredulously. "How could you have done that to me?"

Carl responded, "It's the truth. He had hired a lawyer who had informed this law officer that all communication should go through her. I was only being courteous informing him of the arson, no evidence of any bodies of his family, and no evidence of the Buick – the only thing that he was actually concerned about."

Blair decided she would simply explain what she had witnessed at the party and leave. The waitress appeared at that time to take their orders. She ordered an ice tea. Carl ordered a martini and some hot wings. Blair explained that she had heard raised voices at the party so she had curiously glanced over to see Stanford forcefully grab Julia by the arm jerking her from her sitting position to a standing position at which time she had hit her cheek on his chin for which he had backhanded her. He had then proceeded to drag her from the party all the while she was crying and he was ranting about how she couldn't even act appropriately at the party.

After completing her recital, she stood and informed Carl that he would have to cover the check as she was leaving. Now it was Carl's turn to look incredulous as he could not believe that she had had the balls to ask him out for drinks and appetizers and then left sticking him with the bill!

He needed to eat at least a little something before going to interrogate Stanford at the local police station so he waited for the drinks and wings to arrive and asked for the check so that his tab was clear when he did leave.

CHAPTER 14

He arrived at the police station just after they had completed Stanford's processing. He was sitting at the desk awaiting transport to night court for arraignment. They didn't mind when Carl asked if he could ask him a few questions in one of the interrogation rooms as it would delay his ability to go to court until the next day. They had had to deal with his whining and nastiness since they had arrested him. For someone who was losing everything, you would think that the poor guy would know when to keep his mouth shut.

Carl asked Stanford if he could get him something to drink which Stanford turned down. "How were things at home prior to the explosion?"

"Fine!"

"You were having some money problems according to your credit report, bank balances, and getting ready to lose the family home. Didn't that bother you?"

"That's none of your business!"

"Weren't you getting ready to lose the Buick to the bank as well?"

"Screw you!"

"You can continue to answer with these nonanswers or you can try to help me find out who did this to you and your family. If I am able to find out who is responsible for this tragedy, it will free up the insurance funds faster. That would allow you to purchase those new tires or car."

"What do you want to know?" Stanford asked with his head hung down despairingly.

"Tell me how things were prior to the explosion. Were you and Julia fighting about money? Did you want to kill her?"

"NO! I didn't want to kill her. My God, man! Why would you think that? Yah, we were experiencing some hard times. Nothing that we hadn't weathered before. We had come to the conclusion that we were going to have to downsize the home and our housing costs overall. We had just worked out a repayment arrangement with both the credit card companies as well as the mortgage company. That was something Julia worked extremely hard to complete. We were going to be tight for about a year but we would have made it."

"Were you upset that you couldn't spend money on things that you wanted to like before?"

"No. It was inevitable. I had come to realize that even before Julia had called the credit card companies and the mortgage company."

"Then why are you so upset about not getting your insurance payments now?"

"I am unable to go to work without a vehicle. I can't afford to take any time off but have been given this week off to get things taken care of. How am I going to get tires for the truck if I can't afford to buy them?"

"What about Julia and the kids?"

"What can I do? They're dead! What do you expect of me?"

At this point, Carl was unsure if he wanted to push Stanford any more. He thanked Stanford for his time. Asked him to wait for the policeman to escort him back to his cell and left informing the policeman that he was done with the interrogation.

He hurried back to his own office to put these facts upon his crime board to see how it impacted the investigation. Unfortunately he was unable to concentrate on his board. He went home, drank a beer, and went straight to bed.

CHAPTER 15

He was awakened early the next morning with knocking on the door. He quickly donned something and answered the door. It was his deputy, George.

"There's been another explosion. This time it was at the Down and Out Motel. It apparently started at a truck which we haven't identified as of yet. It did some minor damage to the building. There were no apparent victims."

"Give me five minutes to shower and change and I will be there."

Carl rapidly jumped into the shower, dressed, and ran out to the jeep. He had actually taken about 20 minutes plus the drive to the Down and Out Motel where Stanford had a room but had spent the night courtesy of the police. Wondering whose truck had been blown up; he strolled over to the area. He was introduced to the night clerk. He asked whose vehicle had been blown up. The night clerk said it belonged to the jerk that had had his tires slit the day before. He couldn't understand why after getting his tires slit, someone would want to blow the entire truck up.

That confirmed that it was Stanford's truck. But like the night clerk, he was having trouble understanding who would bother to blow the truck up after slitting all four tires. He quickly assessed the area for damage or potential victims. There was very minimal damage to the motel structure as it was quite deteriorated in the first place. There were no victims. He asked if anyone had found the trigger device. No one had found the trigger device as of yet.

No one had witnessed anyone approaching the truck yesterday, last night or just before the explosion. If anyone had witnessed this, they weren't going to step forward and state it.

He would have his deputy, George, to canvas the neighborhood again to see if there were any stones left unturned. That was something that George would really appreciate after being awakened at such at an early hour. Meanwhile, he was going to look at recent overnight guests at the Down and Out Motel to see if anyone triggered further investigation. He would also ask if they had paid with credit cards, made copies of identification, and where there actual residences. The night clerk asked if he had a warrant before he released any information. Funny question from the night clerk almost like he had something to hide made it imperative that he stand there while obtaining the search warrant for all of the premises, vehicles, belongings, and any paperwork or records. That took almost 15 minutes where the night clerk was beginning to get a little antsy as he had been restricted from leaving Carl's side.

Upon deliverance of the search warrant the night clerk appeared even more uncomfortable. Carl decided it would be best if he kept the night clerk busy with staying by putting him inside of the cop car so that he couldn't prevent discovery of what he was trying to cover up. Thus, he placed him in the back of George's vehicle so that he couldn't exit nor be let out by anyone other than George. He explained the situation to George who decided he was right about locking up the night clerk. Then the two of them started the search with the assistance of the police force.

After six hours digging into the Down and Out Motel records, current residents, and their belongings, it seemed like it was a bust. Then a car had burned rubber trying to leave the parking lot quickly. He barely managed to get a glimpse of it. It was a newer model blue sedan with someone driving it recklessly. He thought the last three digits of the license plate were _ _ _ G 3 Z. He called the license plate in to see if it would trigger anything.

It was then he allowed the night clerk to get out and leave. He returned to his office somewhat dejected with the complete lack of results from the search other than the reckless sedan.

CHAPTER 16

There were 700 license plates ending with G3Z and 532 were on blue sedans. Restricting the search to newer models reduced it to 243. That would mean a lot more legwork as he looks at each of the owner's names to see if they might fit the possibility of being in the parking lot today. The night clerk denied knowledge of who was in the vehicle, but he suspected that he indeed did know who it might have been and may have been the reason the night clerk had been so nervous. Thinking about that, he decided to send George to where the night clerk lived to see if he may find out what he was so nervous about or see that blue sedan. In the meantime, he had a lot of calls to make to the individual sedan owners to see where they were this morning.

He had spent ten hours on the phone forgetting to eat until Candi had brought him in a sandwich. George had been unsuccessful at locating the night clerk as well. George had waited for hours without the night clerk returning home which according to his neighbors was unusual. They had also shared he had a new girlfriend who drove a newer model blue sedan. They had also shared his habits had seemed to change after meeting this new girlfriend. So, despite not catching the night clerk and his new girlfriend, George had stumbled onto more pieces to this puzzle.

The puzzle needed updating, so Carl started adding more information to the board. The board would be the key to the entire puzzle if only he could see how each of the pieces fit together. George was looking at the board when he commented on the fact that Julia, the kids, and the Buick were missing and unaccounted for.

Carl explained he was waiting for the women's shelters to hopefully call back with some confirmation that she had been spirited away to another area. He was yet to hear back from any of them.

It was at that moment that the phone rang. It was the supervisor for the abuse hotline. She stated there hadn't even been any contact from Julia, the kids, nor had any of the women's shelters offered her any form of assistance.

Now looking at the board, it was beginning to look as if there were multiple things going on. If the house had blown up because of something Stanford had done, then why had Stanford's tires been slit and then the truck blown up? Yet, Stanford could have been guilty of the house and someone else for the tires and truck. The most likely suspect was Julia and they had not found her as of yet. Unless, she was the night clerk's new girlfriend, and that meant they only needed to put surveillance on the night clerk to follow his movements.

Carl turned to Candi and asked if she might be interested in performing a stakeout at the Down and Out Motel to see if she could catch sight of the car, girlfriend, or anything else that might appear suspicious. She was interested and said she could secretively take pictures of anything that might be able to help with solving this crime. She asked if she should call him if anything popped up. He informed her it was imperative that she call for something suspicious.

He had forgotten his list of 243 sedan owners. He had only gone through half of the list when they had updated and collaborated on the board. It was closing time, he decided he would save the rest of the phone call until the morning when he glanced down. A single name caught his interest immediately. Schotts, Stanford and Julia owned a 2007 four door blue Buick sedan with the license plate ZZR G3Z.

He decided to take a picture of the crime board, load it on his computer, and look at these things over pizza and a beer at home. He asked George if he wanted to come over while Candi did recognizance at the Down and Out Motel. George declined stating his wife was pissed that he hadn't been home in the last 18 hours.

Chapter 17

Meanwhile, Stanford had been released on bail. He was steamed. Now, it was impossible to take the cheapest route of buying four new tires. How was he going to keep his job, get a new lawyer as the entire firm wanted nothing to do with him, and survive until he got some money?

He had the deputy let him off at the Down and Out Motel only to be told he was no longer welcome there. Crap! Now where was he going to go? He only had $200 until his next pay day if he still had a job.

He called Jessie who offered him the garage. Janice was unwilling to let him in the house as she was sure he had actually blown up his own house and killed his family. If she believed that it was hard to believe that he was even welcome in her garage. It was probably Jessie standing up to her for him. Since he was in no place to complain, he accepted her gracious offer of a place to stay.

He could let the police know tomorrow where to find him. In the meantime, he had a bed to sleep in at Jessie's garage. Jessie was on the way to pick him up. Since Jessie also worked near the bus yard, he was willing to drop him off and pick him up on his way home each day until he could get some money. Jessie told him he could repay him when he got the money. Of course, that money would go straight into Janice's account, not Jessie's, but that was their problem, not his.

Tonight he could at least sleep without keeping an eye open for any perpetrators.

CHAPTER 18

Carl spent many hours wound up after his discovery that Stanford and Julia owned a car just like the one he was looking for. He looked at the board in earnest. He had projected the image of the board on to his wall to see it in large detail. He really needed to connect the pieces as he put them together.

With this in mind he decided to put together the board on his Visio program. It allowed him to move the items at will without having to redraw the board at any time.

In the center, he placed the Schotts, Stanford, Julia, Jasper, and Catherine. Above that, he placed the explosion at their house indicating arson. No victims and no location for the Buick, Julia, Jasper, or Catherine. Stanford had been at work driving the school bus when the explosion had occurred.

To the right of center, he placed Julia. He put a circle below her for Jasper and another one for Catherine. To Julia's right, he put an oval with question mark next to Gregory, the night clerk.

To the left of center, he placed the Buick. Beneath it included its license plate. Beneath that description, he wrote it was similar to one leaving the Down and Out Motel recklessly after the truck explosion. He also included 243 in the area licensed with the last three digits G3Z.

At this point, he jotted down to the far right that he needed to investigate Gregory further.

Then he went back to realigning the material on the crime board. Beneath the center circle, he placed Stanford. He put down he was at work when house exploded, questionable arsonist, arrested for assaulting Blair, then fired as a client from her law firm. He placed a circle to the bottom left of Stanford with the truck. He put two circles under it. One described the tires being slit. The other described the truck explosion while Stanford was in jail.

Next to the truck circle, he placed a circle for coworkers' opinions. Next to that circle, he placed one for neighbors' opinions. Next to that circle he placed his family past. The last circle was the party at which he had dragged Julia from.

The only coworker spoken to was his supervisor, Ralph, who respected him as a punctual reliable worker. He needed to inquire about Stanford from more of his coworkers. He would try to rectify that tomorrow. If he did it tomorrow, it would still be while Stanford was off until next week per Ralph's suggestion.

Neighbors' opinions differed as far as night and day. Josh said Stanford was hard to get to know and was unsure if he could have created the explosion. Sally said he hadn't come in for coffee on the morning of the explosion as he always did. Stanford had complained about his lack of money for which he blamed Julia. Sally didn't think he could have caused the explosion. Justin didn't think Stanford was smart enough nor had enough desire to do something like that. Anastacia had been concerned about Julia's welfare since she thought Stanford was abusive and capable of causing the explosion for insurance monies. Harry had thought there might have been something strange at the house, but hadn't had any real alarm bells going off. He had yet to speak to the neighbors who had also lost their home or the ones on the corner. He made a not to do that as well.

When looking at family relations and relationships, he hadn't found anything blaring other than the kids beginning to have trouble at school. Their son, Jasper, had multiple behavioral problems noted at school. Both Jasper and Catherine's grades had dramatically declined recently. Julia had quit her job approximately nine months ago although it sounded like the Mayo Clinic was going to let her go for too many personal problems interfering with her capability to work.

That was not all though. According to Blair, Abner, Cory, Harry, and Larry, there was more than one viewpoint on a recent party that both Stanford and Julia had attended. Blair was the only one who stated that Stanford had been abusive to Julia whereas Abner, Cory, Harry, and Larry had all denied any abuse. Kind of makes you wonder if their relationships needed evaluation for abusive tendencies as well.

Okay, he had found some key holes that needed further evaluation to finish up this investigation. First, he needed to talk to Stanford's coworkers. Second, he needed to interview more neighbors. Third, he needed to investigate Gregory further. Last, but not least, he needed to find that blue sedan which he hoped would be Julia's.

CHAPTER 19

S peaking of both Julia and Gregory reminded Carl that
he hadn't heard anything from Candi at the stakeout.
Rather than let her have complete autonomy as he knew
she desired, he called her to check in with how it was going.
Candi informed him that she had seen Gregory come to
work walking from two blocks away. She had not seen
anyone suspicious visiting the office, nor had she had any
signs of the blue sedan.

He asked how she was holding up, did she need a break?
Did he need to take over for the night? She was adamant
that she appreciated the opportunity to act as a deputy and
didn't want his help if he would just allow her to complete
this night's stakeout.

Since Candi seemed to have the stakeout under control,
he decided to take some time to rest.

CHAPTER 20

Stanford was shacked out in Jessie's garage. It might be a little cool out in the garage, but he felt much safer there than he had at the Down and Out Motel. He fell asleep so fast and slept hard.

He was rudely awakened with strange noises. He was having trouble trying to figure out what that noise was. It sounded like a squeaking rocking chair when someone too heavy was sitting in it and rocking. He didn't have anything like that in the garage. Jessie didn't have anything like that in the house either. Besides, it was still the middle of the night. Since the garage was only a single story, there was nothing overhead that was creating that noise. That left something outside making that noise.

He turned on the light, put on some pants, and found a flashlight then proceeded to check outside for any obvious causes of the noise. When he opened the door, it was much heavier than when he had entered earlier in the evening. In fact, he was having great trouble opening it much further than the six inches he had opened it thus far. It was then that he noticed the horrendous gasoline and kerosene smell. Oh my God! Was someone trying to set Jessie's garage on fire? Didn't they know someone was in there? He started shouting for help at the same time that he heard that big "WOOP" as the fire was lit. He kept yelling trying to make as much noise as he could to try and wake the neighbors or Jessie or Janice. He was too close to the heat so he had to move to the center of the room to try and get away from the heat. He kept yelling until he had no oxygen left at which time he passed out. Minutes after he passed out, the natural gas tank exploded outside which awakened the neighborhood. Everyone looked outside and picked up the phone to call 911.

Unfortunately for Stanford, the arrival of the fire trucks and ambulance was too late to save him or the garage. They did salvage some of Jessie's home when they got the fire under control. However, Jessie's home was uninhabitable.

Janice kept repeating that she should never have allowed that monster to come back to their property. She was already blaming him for setting the fire and thought it was justice that he probably perished in the fire.

The fire inspector asked who the monster was. "Stanford Schotts!" He picked up the phone and called Carl to inform him what had happened as well as a potential dead body in the center of the garage. It would be some time before the body could be positively identified as Stanford Schotts, but it seemed he was the most likely victim.

CHAPTER 21

Carl was rudely awakened with a phone call at three am. This was the third phone call in a week from Stanley, the fire inspector, about an explosion and fire. This was getting old. The problem with this one was that it appeared that Stanford may have perished in this one. That meant he was not going to be easy to hold accountable for the first explosion and fire. Damn!

It was another early morning attempting to deal with things. He called Candi to see how her stakeout was going. He could tell she was sleeping just by the fact that she was having great difficulty paying attention to him. That meant she had unlikely noticed anything after talking to him earlier in the evening. That wouldn't help him to try and put pieces together. He asked her if she could obtusely check to see if Gregory was working, or if he had someone with him right now like Julia.

While he waited on her to check this out, he took his shower, got dressed and started over to Jessie's house. On the drive to Jessie's house, Candi called back. She had found Gregory sound asleep at the desk. His car parked in the parking lot. No one with him, in his car, or the blue sedan suspected of foul play.

He was still tired, despite the shower. Stanley was not the least considerate. "What took you so long? Seems to me that you should have this routine down by now!"

Carl hadn't quite expected to have Stanley attack him upon his arrival at the crime scene. Yet, Stanley had been here at least 45 minutes longer than he had which meant he was missing more sleep than Carl. So Carl decided to give Stanley a break about his bad mood.

"I had to check on something prior to coming to the crime scene. It has helped to rule out at least one suspect for this scene. It has however raised the issue of where some of the other players are at. What do you have for me so far?"

Stanley was not the least bit contrite about biting off Carl's head. He responded, "The fire was deliberately started using gasoline and kerosene as fuel for the fire. There was only the one victim, presumed to be Stanford Schotts until positively identified upon autopsy. It seems like he tried to exit, but then tried to go to the center of the room away from the heat to try and survive longer. That may have actually reduced the heat, but actually increased his exposure to the gases that were accumulating. The Brooks, Jessie and Janice, suffered a lot of property damage, but didn't get hurt. Janice has been blaming Stanford for starting the fire since the arrival of emergency personnel. She still hasn't acknowledged that someone had moved the heavy chest in front of the only exit besides the garage door which apparently hasn't been operational for the last six months per Jessie. Go figure. You would think that she could see reason. My take is she really didn't like Stanford and resented Jessie allowing him the opportunity to stay in their garage."

"Thanks, Stanley. Let me know any updates as you get them. Could you point out Jessie and Janice Brooks?"

Stanley pointed to a couple holding on to one another while she was sobbing on his shoulder. Carl quietly approached the couple. He was contemplating how to start. Should he offer condolences on the death of a friend? Would it be better to offer condolences on the loss of their house? Offer some assistance with housing during their time of need? He decided to offer his condolences on their loss and let them interpret that in the method that they would.

Janice looked at him with blank eyes when he introduced himself and offered his condolences. She asked him what she had done to expect such a catastrophic event to occur. She was unsure of what to expect from the world as a whole. She then began to shake uncontrollably. He called the medics over to assist her with her obvious shock.

He stood by with Jessie as the medics offered and then gave her something to help with sedation. The medic suggested she spend the night in the hospital to insure that if she awakened with the same symptoms, she could be properly taken care of. Jessie agreed and then proceeded to climb into the ambulance to ride with her and spend the night in the hospital as well. Carl let Jessie know he would talk to the two of them at a later time and to take care of Janice right now.

He decided to ask which of the neighbors had called in the fire. After finding out which ones had made the calls, he started asking questions to each.

Brett is the elderly man who lived directly across the street. He had awakened because he thought he had heard a loud noise. But, it had not recurred. He thought everything was okay and decided to go back to sleep. Then he had heard the loud explosion. He had immediately awakened, grabbed his coat, the portable phone, and went to the window while dialing 911. He had immediately seen the flames across the street. He rushed over to see if he could help Jessie and Janice out of the home. They are a nice couple and he didn't want them to get hurt if they hadn't awakened with the explosion. By the time he had crossed the street they had made it out of the house. Janice had been screaming at Jessie about allowing that monster to stay in their garage and now he had started the fire that had caused the explosion. Brett had been unaware that anyone was in the garage. Whoever, if anyone, was in the garage had long since expired. He was not a hero and would not start acting like one now.

Carl asked if he had looked at the clock when he had heard the first loud sound or if knew what the loud sound had been. Brett denied knowing either. Carl then moved on to questioning the next neighbor who had called it in.

Gerilyn and Douglas lived next door to Jessie and Janice. They had awakened with the loud boom of the natural gas tanks. They had run out to see what had gone on. Then Gerilyn had called 911 while Douglas went over to Jessie and Janice's house to see what he could do to help them. Like Brett, he had been unaware that anyone was housed in the garage until he had heard Janice screaming at Jessie that the monster was responsible for setting the fire and she hoped he had perished in the fire. Goodness, Janice must really not have like Stanford. Gerilyn was not aware of anything other than what Douglas had just shared.

The last neighbor who had called it in was Sherry who lived next to Brett. She denied hearing any loud noise prior to the explosion, but had been awakened at 2:15 am because of the start of one of those scooter things. She had attempted to find who had been stupid and rude enough to start one of those things at that hour. However, all she got was a glimpse of someone small in stature wearing what looked like a sweatshirt with a hood and blue jeans as they had driven away in the opposite direction as what Jessie and Janice's home was located. She didn't interpret their driving fast as if fleeing the crime. Since she had looked out the side window of her bedroom, she had not noticed the fire immediately. She had however, noticed a bright light and wondered if it was a full moon as she had not noticed prior to going to sleep. Just as she was getting back into bed, she had heard the explosion. She immediately called 911 and had not even attempted to leave her home until she had dressed to make sure she was not seen in anything less than appropriate attire. Carl thanked her for her information and asked if she thought she could identify the driver of the scooter or the scooter. She had stated that she had noticed the scooter was a dark color but beyond that she could not positively identify it.

Carl then asked who had been first on the scene. Once again, it was Greg Chowdry and Terry Sample, the firefighters who were first on the scene of the original explosion and fire. They were frustrated and wondered if Carl had actually created the potential for this explosion by asking everyone to keep quiet about the lack of bodies at the first explosion as well as creating the scenario that Stanford may have been to blame setting him up for possible retaliation from someone. Carl couldn't blame them for that perception as he was feeling a little guilty about it as well. But he got back to the business at hand and asked what their interpretations of the situation were. They informed him that someone had deliberately set the fire, moved a large storage box in front of the only functioning doorway, and had left Stanford in there to expire. It had taken them mere minutes to salvage what little of the house that they could, but they had protected other homes from being destroyed this time. Then they had stated he needed to get a better handle on his investigation as it appeared to be getting beyond his control.

Chapter 22

Carl received a phone call just then from Candi and decided it was a good time to break away. He was only too glad to get away from the negative atmosphere as well as the guilt that he was feeling. He asked Candi what was up. She informed him that she was glad he had awakened her. She had immediately seen a scooter slide around to the back of the Down and Out Motel. She was unsure if she should go investigate further since he had said to call him if anything happened that needed further evaluation. He informed Candi to keep her eyes open and he would be over quickly to investigate who that may have been. While he was getting into the jeep, he asked her if Gregory was still sleeping at the desk. She stated she was unsure, but the desk lamp had been turned out soon after the scooter had appeared. Then, he actually started to wonder if she had immediately seen the scooter, why she had waited so long to call him. Then he looked down at his cell phone to discover it was on silent and he had had three missed calls from Candi.

He arrived at the Down and Out Motel minutes later. He hadn't glanced at his watch when he left Jessie and Janice's home. But, he could look and see what time he had received and answered Candi's phone call. He looked at his cell phone for the time now and the time he had received Candi's phone call. It had taken him twenty minutes to get here. He then looked at the time when Candi had first tried to call him and he had missed it. He subtracted twenty minutes and it was 2:22 am. What time had Sherry said she had been rudely awakened by a scooter? That's right, about 2:15 am. Things were finally beginning to add up. Now all he had to do was first find the scooter, identify it. Then he would try to find the perpetrator who had been driving it.

He decided in the scheme of things, he needed to park out of site of the office to be able to quietly snoop for the scooter which Candi stated had pulled around to the back. He quietly closed the Jeep door and started walking sedately back to the back of the building. This was one of the dirtiest neighborhoods around and it certainly lived up to its reputation tonight. It smelled of garbage, waste, sex, and neglect. He tried desperately not to get his shoes too dirty while walking behind the building. It was definitely dark out, but he was hesitant to use the flashlight he had in his pocket. He didn't want to give the scooter owner any advance notice of his arrival if he could keep from it.

It took him almost thirty minutes to make it around the back of the building. He had not found the scooter. He went back to behind the office and called Candi. He asked her to try and enter the office to speak to Gregory.

Candi went to the office. She rang the bell to have someone come and respond to her. She waited five minutes of intermittently ringing the bell without any response. She called Carl to tell him there was no response and didn't seem to be anyone at the desk. He asked her if it would be easy to get behind the desk and move towards the back. She said it appeared fairly easy. He told her to go ahead and try to come out the back way being careful to act like she was just trying to find someone to help her with getting a room for her and her boyfriend. Minutes later she was standing in front of Carl in the back never once seeing or hearing Gregory or the scooter in the back room. She had checked the bathroom in the back room and no one was there as well. That meant that Gregory was missing now as well as Julia, Jasper, and Catherine. Stanford was presumed dead. There had been three explosions, a blue sedan similar to Julia and Stanford's seen at the scene of the second explosion, and a scooter seen at the third that was now missing.

He put out an APB on Gregory, Julia, and a 2007 four door blue Buick sedan with the license plate ZZR G3Z. They had at least a forty minute head start if they had disappeared when Candi had first noticed the scooter. He sent Candi home and told her to take the rest of the day off. He then went into the office to update his crime board. The missing pieces were getting smaller, but also more difficult to find.

CHAPTER 23

Carl started searching the internet for any additional information he could find on Gregory Hascott, the night clerk, Julia Schotts, Jasper Schotts, Catherine Schotts, Jessie Brooks, Janice Brooks and any connections to any of the others. He would ask George to interview Stanford's coworkers about Stanford, his family, how things were going for the Schotts, the Schotts' neighbors, their opinions of the family, their relationships, who they suspected of these explosions, and anything they could remember preceding the events that had transpired.

Meanwhile, Carl had found some information on the computer that he should have found earlier in his searches. Jasper had a juvenile record. Why hadn't he found that before? Did he just overlook it because he was so much in favor of blaming Stanford? Looking at the information,

Jasper had been arrested for possession of drug paraphernalia. He had been sentenced to a drug treatment center where he had spent the standard three months of treatment before being allowed to return to his home situation. He should have George check out the drug treatment center to see what there might be that could connect some of these dots. There had been no new charges against Jasper since that time. Upon further review of the behavioral issues and his grades dropping, these started occurring around the time that he had went to the drug treatment center. Usually these occurred prior as sort of a warning of upcoming problems. Yet, it didn't occur that way with Jasper. His grades started dropping with behavioral problems at school after his release from the drug treatment center. He should remember to ask George to ask if there seemed to be problems with Jasper's behaviors at the treatment center.

Catherine didn't trigger the same findings. Her grades had started falling at the time that Jasper had entered the drug treatment center. What was it about Jasper entering the drug treatment center that would cause her grades to drop? Her teachers might shed some light on that. He needed to have George ask the teachers if Catherine had shared any useful information.

Julia had not had anything in her past that pointed to problems. At least, not at first glance. Upon further review, it may be that she may have contributed to her son's drug problem. There had been an official complaint that had led to a sanction placed upon her nursing license preventing the use or distribution of any narcotic substances. That was unusual for a medical professional unless there had been a history of substance abuse. Healthcare professionals were known to be amongst the highest substance abusers secondary to the availability of said substances. She had quit her job at the same time that Jasper had gotten arrested and sent to drug treatment nine months previously. Was it her drug use? Jasper's? How did her job loss fit into this scenario? If George had time, he could interview her past coworkers and supervisors at the Mayo Clinic which would probably be the most closed mouth of all interviews with their need to protect their reputation.

Gregory Hascott supposedly never existed. Uh-Oh, this was leading in a totally new direction. He should have taken him in and seriously interviewed him when he had the chance. He would have to try and locate who Gregory Hascott is and was as well as who and / or what he had done in his past. What did he have that Gregory Hascott had touched that he could possibly run fingerprints on? George's car. What time was it? It was 6 am. He could call George into work early and get his car printed STAT. That would be the best method to find out who this Gregory had been. George would be in after his shower.

Jessie Brooks was a normal working American trying to live the American dream. He had graduated high school, worked at the local cable company putting cable lines in as needed, married his high school sweetheart, and settled down outside of Phoenix. His high school sweetheart, Janice Cout Brooks, was also a normal American looking for the American dream. Neither had ever been arrested. Neither stirred any interest about any activities, nor had any complaints from anyone about them. Although they seemed to be saints, he would keep them on the back burner because saints weren't always saints.

As of yet, he hadn't found any additional connections to further improve his understanding of how all of this was going to fit together.

CHAPTER 24

George had made it in. He was not happy to learn his car was going to be temporarily confiscated to have the entire back seat area fingerprinted in an attempt to identify Gregory Hascott. Since his vehicle was confiscated, he decided he would rent a vehicle at the department's expense. His wife was interested in owning a sports car, so he chose to rent the newest Ford Mustang Convertible. Carl was not about to argue especially as George had not even argued.

George requested a ride to the rental car agency and signature on the rental agreement stating the department would be responsible for the fees involved in the rental. Carl was only too happy to oblige. Once that transaction was completed, George went about his various road trips.

He decided to visit Jasper's treatment center first as this was a new twist in the investigation. When he arrived at the treatment center, he was met at the door by a guard who refused to allow him entrance until cleared by the medical director. That was the first time that George had met that much security at the door of a drug treatment center. It took another 45 minutes before he was allowed to be ushered into the medical director's office. Dr. Gaspen, the medical director, was courteous at that time offering him something to drink or eat. They talked about nothing for a few minutes before George was beginning to get a little frustrated with the stalling tactics.

"Do you remember a patient by the name of Jasper Schotts?" George asked expecting the canned response of HIPAA preventing any sharing of patient's names or medical conditions.

Instead, he received a positive response that Jasper had attended a court ordered drug treatment program. Then Dr. Gaspen informed him he could not tell him anything more than he had as it would be considered confidential information protected under HIPAA practices. George asked if there was anything about the family that had triggered any concerns about his discharge into his home environment. Dr. Gaspen avoided the question stating HIPAA. George asked if he knew anyone by the name of Gregory Hascott. Jessie Brooks? Janice Brooks? Had he ever treated Julia? Stanford? Catherine? Again, he was prevented from finding out any additional information. Dr. Gaspen went on to explain that even if he were to come back with warrants, he would be unable to discern any information that would be useful.

Two hours wasted in the driving, waiting, and questioning only to get what he had expected all along. Well, maybe he could catch one of the employees leaving for the day and ask them if they knew anything.

He was in luck, apparently, they were a little more proactive with work schedules and had staggered working schedules so that there was always someone available to watch the patients. She seemed to be by herself, something that was desirable as far as George was concerned. That way if she was unaware of HIPAA, he could possibly find out some information.

"Excuse me, could you help me for just a minute?"

"What can I do for you officer?"

"I am interested in a young man by the name of Jasper who was a patient here six to nine months ago. Was he a problem? Did he share any information about his family? Did Gregory Hascott ever visit Jasper? What about a Jessie or Janice Brooks?"

"Do you have a picture of any of them?"

George pulled out pictures. He first showed her Jasper who she easily recognized. She pointed out Gregory Hascott as George Henry, one of their night housekeepers who was let go approximately seven months ago. She didn't recognize either Jessie or Janice. George thanked her for her help.

He got in the car and left. He called Carl to let him know what he had found out. When he hung up, he called the Down and Out Motel and asked how long Gregory Hascott had been employed. The manager said he had been an employee for the last month. When asked what kind of reference check he had performed, the manager was a little cheeky with his response, but it amounted to very little in the way of a background check. That added another layer of doubt about who Gregory or George was and how he played into the scenario.

One more interesting piece of information that would assist in nailing the coffin shut. Yet, just how to finish the connection between Jasper and Gregory or George or whoever his name was, how that would play into these explosions, Stanford's murder, the disappearance of Julia, Catherine, and Jasper. Well, he decided he might find some additional information at Jasper's and Catherine's schools, his next two stops.

He stopped at Catherine's school next as it was closer to the treatment center where he had been. He went to the office and asked if he could get some information on two of their students, Jasper and Catherine Schotts. The clerk immediately called the superintendent to ask permission to share any details regarding these two students. Apparently that would be limited as he was immediately ushered into the superintendent's office.

The superintendent was evasive initially. However, George decided to discuss the easy subject of their recent grades, past grades, and if any of the teachers had any complaints about behaviors or concerns about these two students. The superintendent shared that Catherine had recently had some trouble with her grades, but that no teachers had had any behavioral problems or concerns that they had shared with the superintendent. Since her teachers were in with students at this time, it was not a good time to talk with them. She would ask each of them personally and get back to him if any had any concerns about Catherine. She attempted to shoo him out of the office at that time completely avoiding the subject of Jasper.

George was not so easily avoided. He asked her how Jasper's grades and behavior had been prior to that. She gave him an annoyed look but then sat back down. She took a deep breath, let it out very slowly.

She just sat there for a few minutes as if trying to decide what, how much, or if she would continue to deny anything. Then she grimaced as if she was going to do something extremely painful. She opened her mouth, hesitated, and then closed it once again. George thought it best to just wait and let her come to grips with what it was she was trying to say-if he pushed too much she might take the narrow path that was standard and he wouldn't find out anything. More time passed and then out of the blue, she volunteered, "Jasper was originally a very bright, happy, child. As he progressed towards his middle school years, he became increasingly aggressive towards other children, then some of the teachers, and finally me. We actually banned him from stepping on to the campus, even for any of Catherine's functions. We made a referral to children's services for psychiatric evaluation and support, not just for Jasper, but for Julia and Catherine as well. I can't remember the last time that Stanford came to any activities or parent meetings. He quit around the same time that Jasper's behaviors began to change. Jasper's grades actually had begun to decline well after the behaviors began. That is all I am able to share with you. Now, if you don't mind, I have a school to run and you are infringing on my ability to concentrate my efforts upon it."

With that she stood up, went to the door, opened it, and waited until George got up, thanking her for her time, and left. The door was forcefully shut immediately after he exited her office. It was immediately apparent that that was all he was going to get from her.

Since it was getting late and he had had no lunch, he went back to the office to meet up with Carl. When he arrived, Carl was more than glad to discuss what George had found out. Carl also let George know he could have his car. They had found many fingerprints, most of whom they had already matched to individuals that had been arrested by either Carl or George. They had about ten more fingerprints to match before they would have a definite identification of Gregory or George or whoever he was.

Carl also updated George on what he had found out about the individuals from his talking with the neighbors again, Stanford's coworkers, the local grocery market employees, the coaches at the after school programs which was nothing that they didn't already know. They started discussing the situation and found that they had some major concerns. The first concern being that Jasper seemed to have some violent tendencies. The second would be that he had been at the treatment center at the same time as Gregory or George was an employee. The scooter had been seen at the scene of the third explosion and again at the Down and Out Motel where Gregory or George had been an employee. Now, there was still no sign of Jasper, Catherine, or Julia. But there had been the blue sedan with the same last three digits of the license plate as Julia and Stanford's Buick.

They looked at the fingerprints that remained unmatched to see if they could try to pinpoint who had been in the back of George's vehicle that they had not pressed charges against. At the same time, they put those ten remaining prints into the national FBI, CIA, and TSA databases in an attempt to find someone else. Within minutes, there were names spitting out all over the place for a single set of prints. Then the phone rang.   It was the FBI.

CHAPTER 25

They wanted to know why the prints had been collected. Carl explained they had had three explosions, one homicide, and four missing individuals and they were trying to close the case. The FBI agent stated someone would be there at nine am tomorrow to discuss the case with them. That was not what Carl or George wanted, but didn't see what other options they had. They decided to call it a night and see what tomorrow would bring.

CHAPTER 26

The good news was that Carl had not received any early morning phone calls with reports of another explosion. That did not negate the fact that the FBI was coming in this morning and may take over his case which he had fought so early on to keep within the sheriff's department. Well, he had better shower, drink his coffee, eat something, and make it to work a little early.

When he made it to the office he was a little surprised to learn that the FBI was waiting in his office for him. It was only 7:30. They had set the meeting for nine. He made his way into the office to find the FBI agent sitting at his desk as if he were in charge. Carl was not going to let the meeting start out feeling as if he had already lost control. "Would you mind getting out of my SEAT?"

The FBI agent stood, came around the desk, extended his hand for a hand shake, "Good morning, my name is Malcolm Dride with the FBI."

"Carl Jansten, sheriff."

"Do you want to bring me up to snuff with the case?"

"Do you want to tell me why the FBI is interested in this particular case? Why would you call me when I accessed your fingerprint records? What is the importance of my case to what you want or are trying to keep me from finding?"

Malcolm stood and went over to the board. He pointed to the first arson. "Who caused this?"

Carl was not happy to let him try to take over. "Once again, why is the FBI interested in what is going on? I didn't call you. You called us."

"Once you tell me what is going on, I can let you know what I think you need to know."

"I guess we're done." Carl said as he opened the door and motioned for Malcolm to leave. Malcolm sit down, and folded his arms instead of leaving as Carl had indicated.

Carl closed the door. Then he sat down waiting on Malcolm to tell him something that would allow him to give some. They sat there calmly for thirty minutes pretending to outwait the other, both growing more frustrated by the minute. Then, George knocked and entered. "Oh. I didn't know they were still here."

Carl motioned for George to come on in. He introduced him to Malcolm. "I've been waiting on Malcolm to explain how the FBI is involved in this case. He has yet to explain past the stereotypical need to know phrase."

George turned to Malcolm with an expectant look upon his face. Malcolm reiterated his need to be brought up the present with the case before sharing any details. George decided to take a different tactic with Malcolm than Carl's. He asked who Gregory Hascott was. No response from

Malcolm. George Henry? Gary Hansen? Geoffrey Hord? Gaylen Hish? Giles Hayberry? Gantry Hand? That got a little sparkle from Malcolm's eyes or at least George thought it had. "Gantry Hand must be someone that you are familiar with. Should we run his name through the computer to find out what kind of interest you may have in him?"

Malcolm decided it was time to let them see a little bit of his information in an attempt to finish this as soon as possible. Malcolm shared that Gantry had been a lad in New York City during the Twin Towers explosion. He had been someone that seemed to have a lot of information to share to various individuals after the explosions. Then when the FBI had become interested in what he had been sharing with various emergency personnel and news persons, he had disappeared off the face of the earth. They had been able to track someone with the same prints through various cities across the United States. Yet, each time they had come close to finding him to interview him about what he knew about the Twin Towers bombings, he would disappear once again. It seemed like he had done the same thing once again.

Carl then asked how old he estimated this Gantry would be today if he were estimating his age. Malcolm stated he would be about 40-45 years old. This definitely fit with Gregory Hascott's age. George whipped out the picture of Gregory to see if Malcolm recognized him. Malcolm thought it might be Gantry given the prints were a perfect match. Carl asked what their plans were if they were able to find Gantry. Malcolm said they needed to question him, but he was actually considered a possible terrorist.

Carl decided it might be best to get Malcolm's perceptions of what or who may have set the explosions and where they should take their investigation. If Jasper was as violent as they thought and he was consorting with a suspected terrorist, he may be much more violent than he had originally thought.

Carl went over the crime board with both Malcolm and George. Three hours later, they had discussed the entire board and had come up with a few areas that needed further evaluation. They would work with the FBI to solve their crimes and possibly get more insight into the twin towers explosions at the same time.

Malcolm requested the use of one internet port to access the FBI files to look for potential sites that Jasper, Julia, Catherine, and / or Gantry could escape to. Once they crossed county lines, Carl and George no longer had access to them. However, Malcolm was not restricted to the county, state, or truthfully, the country. This would be the best solution for all. It took Malcolm minutes to find some unknown information about a property in Jasper's name bought approximately ten months ago with cash. It was located just within the county at the base of the South Mountain Park. According to records there were no buildings on the property. It seemed like the logical step to take a short drive out there to see if they might be able to locate any of the missing suspects.

They took two vehicles. It might prove to be useful if they needed to box in a vehicle or in a chase. It took them almost an hour to get there because traffic was congested at that time of the day. Once there, it seemed like it might be a waste until Malcolm stated there was over one hundred acres of wilderness that they would need to search. They started with the access road. Malcolm led the way driving slowly looking right and left for any signs of life as well as the scooter and Buick. They had driven approximately one mile when Malcolm stopped his vehicle. He got out talking with Carl and George to see how they wanted to proceed with searching the rest of the property. Carl stated it seemed like it might be smart to go back to the beginning of the property, park one of the vehicles across the access road to prevent easy entry or leaving. George didn't want to leave his vehicle and Malcolm didn't want to let anyone know they were there if they weren't already aware.

They decided to leave the vehicles where they were and to investigate further on foot. Often, these areas had caves that would not be easily visible unless one was nearby walking. Since the access road was close to the north side of the property, it seemed to make the most sense to move slowly to the south. They spread out approximately twenty feet apart walking towards the mountain side looking for any tracks, clues of recent burials or earth movement, the scooter, or the Buick. It took them an hour to walk to the southern edge of what was perceived to be the property line. They started back parallel to where they had started. This took them another hour. When they reached the vehicles, they took a little break. They had been at this for hours and it was the heat of the day. Carl decided to send George back to the office to get the tent, flood lights, food, water, and cooler to allow them to continue to search through the night and possibly cornering them on this property if indeed they were hiding here. Malcolm agreed with the plan, but put in a call to request additional assistance with looking for other potential sites that may need further investigation.

They decided to wait in the shade provided by Malcolm's vehicle and tried to come up with some ideas of the best method to proceed when George returned to the site with all of the supplies. They decided it would be best if they actually pitched the tent where they currently were as it was close to the access road, away from the entry into the property, and less noticeable.

With these decisions made, they started discussing their private lives to pass the time until George returned. It was then that they started hearing some hammering noises far off in the distance. Rather than try to run and find where the sound was coming from. Malcolm called the local office and requested a crop duster plane to fly by and see if they could locate any areas of activity that they might want to focus their search to. They continued to sit there trying to pinpoint the direction of the sound for their own attempts on the ground once George returns with their supplies.

It was another hour before the crop duster plane flew over. They seemed to make the single pass when Malcolm got the phone call stating there was nothing out there other than brush and sand – no scooter, no Buick, no people other than Malcolm's black SUV. Shortly after, George returned with all of the supplies. They set up the tent, making sure to zip it up well to prevent any snakes, scorpions, or other pests got inside. When they got done with that it was nearing dinner time as well as getting dark – not a good time to start a search. They decided to call it a night and prepped the meal.

As the sun went down, the sunset was magnificent. Then they began to hear the coyotes and wolves howling. It made for a different melody than the bar where Carl would rather have been. He pulled out his laptop, reviewed his crime board while wasting time before hitting the sack. Might as well do so early and start early so that they could make the most of the cool light morning time.

When he was making his last bathroom trip, he noticed what he thought might be some fire off to the southwest. He went back to the tent and asked George and Malcolm to look and see if he was making things up. Both George and Malcolm agreed there was something like a light coming from the southwest, but they would need to draw a map gauging where it was in relation to their camp for investigation in the morning. It might be that the light was coming from a hidden cave sight where Gantry, Jasper, Julia, and Catherine may be hiding out at. They called it a night and would begin where they left off in the morning.

Chapter 27

Four o'clock came awfully early despite being up at that hour or earlier almost every morning for the last two weeks. Carl was the last one to rise. George and Malcolm were drinking a cup of coffee while waiting on him to rise without encouragement from them. Now that he was up and around, they pulled out the breakfast to consume before starting their search.

Three hours later, they had covered another 180 foot strip of land without any sign of any camps. According to the map they had estimated last night, they had at least another half mile or so to get to the lighted area. However, it was not smart to go for the gusto and possibly miss the important information along the way. They continued to look for another three hours. Time to break for lunch – just PB & J with Gatorades and water. They spent about forty-five minutes eating and relaxing before they started the search again. They continued to search until approximately two o'clock and then stopped because the heat was unbearable. Carl took that time to call Candi to see if there had been anything going on that needed his immediate attention. Malcolm called the local office to see if there had been any new developments in the case as well. No updates.

They enjoyed the shade until about five, and then started the search for a short time deciding that they mark their spot along the access road at sunset. Then they would return to the camp for the night. They were able to mark off another 120 foot strips. They marked the spot at the access road with three xxx's five feet apart so that it was not as easy to miss in the morning. They then started their walk back to camp. They saw the light once again at approximately the same spot as the night before making it more certain that they were likely to find a hidden cave at the base of the mountain. They quickly ate more P B & J sandwiches with chips, Gatorades, and water, made their last pit stops then hit the sack.

CHAPTER 28

"What the hell was that?!?!" Carl shouted as an extremely loud rumble was reducing in sound. It actually sounded as if it came from nearby. His next thought was not a good one. What if they hadn't found the Schotts soon enough and Gantry had blown them or himself to smithereens. He rapidly put his clothes on as George and Malcolm were doing the same. He was concerned that they had been too slow or methodical. As soon as he had pants on he was calling for emergency vehicles to respond to the base of the mountain side. Malcolm was also doing the same with the FBI offices. As a team, they exited the tent, got into their vehicles and progressed to the site of the explosion.

When they neared the site, Carl realized it was near the area that they had seen the light the other night. Now he was extremely sorry that he had let Malcolm cloud his desire to immediately start at that site next instead of being methodical. Once again, he had not acted soon enough to prevent another potential tragedy. Too late for such recriminations, it was time to see if there was anything he could save or salvage for his investigation.

With those thoughts fresh in his mind, he pulled George aside once they parked their vehicles and asked that George not speak to or in front of Malcolm. George was more than agreeable to this plan as he had felt left out since Malcolm had seemingly taken over the operation, or at least that was George's perception. They had parked approximately 150 feet back from the site and were proceeding with caution towards the explosion site. As they neared the actual base of the mountain, they found lots of debris with dust blowing slightly at the base. It must have been where the light had come from originally and now was obliterated. Carl, George, and Malcolm all started removing some of the lighter debris while Carl called Candi to ask her to get some heavy equipment and operators to come to the site to help with debris removal. It would expedite the recovery process as well as possibly find any survivors that may still be there.

Carl then made an attempt to look for any clues such as tire tracks, human tracks, and any trails that might lead elsewhere while George and Malcolm continued to work on removing the debris. Carl noticed some tire tracks which he proceeded to take a picture of before the heavy equipment arrived and obliterated that piece of evidence. They looked like car tire tracks to him, but he was not an expert. He had not found any sign of the scooter tracks as of yet. He could hear the emergency vehicles coming and knew that if he was to find any more evidence in the vicinity he would have to find it fast before they arrived.

He was unsuccessful at finding any additional evidence prior to the emergency vehicles arriving. Now they had additional manpower, the removal of the debris was easier, but they still had some rather large boulders that would have to wait on the heavy equipment to arrive. When the front loader started moving the large boulders out of the way, it became evident that this was a planned explosion, and had been limited in its intended scope. It seemed to just close off the entrance to the cave. He hoped that if it had been intended to kill the Schotts, that it was unsuccessful. Just a few more boulders and they might be able to get some light and people in there to scope out the interior of the cave.

There! The whole was big enough for George to make it into the cave with light while the front loader continued to remove more boulders. Greg Chowdry and Terry Sample, firefighters followed George in to see if they could render first aid if needed. George was not too happy to go in, but felt safer once he realized that Greg and Terry were going in right after him.

He immediately noticed what looked like a cave like house with many amenities including interior electricity. This area had been prepped for living for some time prior to all of this occurring. Yet, it was important to find out if there were any survivors- he could look for other significant clues later.

He was probably fifty feet from the opening to the cave, when it veered off into two slightly different directions. That was when it became apparent that they would need to split up or investigate one then return to investigate the other. George sent Greg back to ask for another two to three persons to come in and investigate for potential victims. George's intention was to have additional bodies to also watch at the veering. They could let the other team know if they needed to come to the other side or to prevent someone slipping back to the opposite side unnoticed to escape later in all of the mayhem.

It was only minutes before Carl and Malcolm and two other firefighters showed up to help. Carl decided to go down one side with a team while George went down the other letting Malcolm monitor both sides to see who would need assistance first. They started out carefully as the electricity that was present didn't seem to be working as it was probably knocked out during the explosion.

George had gone another seventy-five feet or so when he noticed a light up ahead. He so wanted to rush towards that light, but knew that he might potentially miss any victims or clues if he went too fast. Greg and Terry had noticed the light ahead as well and commented it was strange to see a light further into the cave as opposed to towards the exit. As they came closer to the light, it became obvious that it was coming from a more superior source. Now, they noticed that it felt like they were also walking at a slight incline. They actually slowed as a team as if afraid of what the light might bring.

It was good thing, just then George noticed a trip wire not more than five feet more barely inches off of the ground. He called a halt to their progress telling both Greg and Terry to be extremely careful of where they were stepping as he could see a trip wire that short distance ahead. Both stopped dead in their tracks. George asked Terry if he would return to see if Malcolm could send some experts ahead that were familiar with Gantry's antics and possible booby traps he may have set before leaving.

It was almost comical watching Terry retreat. If he had been at the battle of Bull Run, he couldn't have made a faster retreat. George patiently surveyed his surroundings since both he and Greg knew it was best to wait as opposed to looking for any potential victims and end up being the victim instead in their haste to assist others in distress.

It seemed like eons before anyone came. They introduced themselves as Darrell and Hannah from the FBI tactical team. They took one look at the trip wire, looked for its source as well as what it might trigger. Hannah noticed the possible ending first. "Thank God you stopped when you did. You would have triggered another explosion and probably disintegrated yourself at the same time."

Now George was feeling a little shaky. They had started out with simple house fire and explosion to multiple explosions, a confirmed murder, and three potential additional victims and no confirmed suspect as of yet. He was concerned that they needed to be real careful as the stakes were rising and they could be next if they were too rushed and rash.

Hannah and Darrell were disassembling the trip wire so that others didn't accidentally set it off either. Once they were done, they looked ahead to see if there were other booby traps. Twenty minutes later, they returned to where Greg and George were waiting to state they had found no more booby traps, no victims.

"However, we found a ladder that led to sunshine, a rocky cliff, and what appeared to be a well worn path to the right of the cliff. We took some pictures then asked Manny to fly over and see if he spotted anything suspicious." Darrell told them. They slowly made their way back to the V to see if Carl had had any more success and to check on the progress at the entrance to the cave.

When they reached the V, Malcolm was not there. Instead, it was one of the ambulance personnel sitting down and waiting on them. He was able to tell them that they had found the body of a man amongst the debris; they suspected it might be Gantry, but would know as soon as the prints were confirmed. He was also able to tell them this place had been used for some time as a home away from home with a large food supply, good water, bathing area, as well as toileting.

CHAPTER 29

While George had been exploring his side, Carl and his team of volunteers had been exploring the other side. They had been gone for quite some time without anyone hearing from then. George decided it was best if someone went to make sure they were okay. He, Greg, Hannah, and Darrell went down the V at a leisurely pace while George contemplated the potential scenarios of what had occurred.

If the man at the entry was Gantry, who had set off the explosion and why? It seemed unlikely that Jasper, Catherine, or Julia were intelligent enough or had enough experience to have set the explosion or the booby trap on the other exit. If it wasn't Gantry, then who was it? Who had been maintaining this place as long as it had been maintained? Who was behind all of this and why? Instead of seeming to find more answers, the more they exposed the more questions that appeared to need answers.

While thinking, George ran straight into the back of Greg who had stopped because Hannah and Darrell were stopped. George looked ahead. The cave once again veered. No one was at the V this time. It seemed like Carl may have split the team up to investigate both sides at the same time, just not with the same back up as before. George sent Greg back to the entrance to bring another five or sic volunteers to investigate and stay at this juncture to see what they could find. Meanwhile, George, Hannah, and Darrell discussed what they had found thus far. George really didn't have much choice but to offer his opinions as they seemed to know more about the case than what he did as well as what he thought Carl knew about the case.

Hannah seemed to think that even though a body had been found at the entrance, they would find that it was not Gantry, but an associate of his from his past. He had probably tripped one of the trip wires when he was trying to escape something or someone and had set of the explosion. Gantry would have known he needed to leave immediately, and would have gathered his captives and made his escape. If they hadn't been afraid of him prior to this, Hannah felt they probably were now.

Darrell disagreed. He thought that the man at the entrance was actually Gantry. He thought that Julia had been using him to accomplish everything she needed accomplished and had planned to dump him all along. She managed to do just that and was even now making her getaway. He argued this made the most sense as this property was in Jasper's name making it less of a likelihood that Gantry was part of this scheme other than to be the stooge instead of using a stooge.

George was almost afraid to share his opinion. He decided to ask some probing questions instead. "What did Gantry have to gain by killing his supposed accomplice? Actually, what did Gantry have to gain from all of these activities? If it was actually Julia, why has she seemed like the dowdy little housewife with the inability to stand up for herself? What was her gain from all of this? She will not get any insurance money. She can't come back to the city as she is a possible suspect and not the victim. Why not have considered someone else like Jessie or Janice who before now have just seemed to be friends? What about one of the kids? Jasper? Catherine? What about the kids ganging up on the adults and literally obliterating all of their problems and then just walking away?"

With his diatribe completed, Darrell seemed to be looking at him as if he wasn't the local yokel. "Why do you think it might be one of the kids or the friends?"

George wasn't too sure if he should share why he thought the kids weren't as saintly as they had been made out to be. "The kids had been having lots of problems as school lately and that usually spells out trouble. It also seems like we often overlook kids saying they're too young to do something like this. Jessie and Janice are just the opposite. They are almost squeaky clean. It's almost like they have no flaws that are visible. It makes me suspicious of them."

"Interesting points." Hannah stated as the new recruits joined them.

George decided he should stay at the V with Greg. He split the remainder up into two teams of five each, Hannah leading one team and Darrell the other.

George was reviewing his thoughts as he was sitting there. Too bad the crime board was back at the camp, he could use it to update the thoughts that were swirling amongst his brain. He pulled out his pocket book and began to make notes. Greg seemed content to doze while waiting to see what would occur next.

CHAPTER 30

Hannah had taken the left V. She and her team had barely gone 100 feet when they run into a snag. There was Carl and Kerry lying on the side of the caves with blood on their faces. She immediately sent one of the rescuers back to change places with Greg to see what they could do to help them as well as to send reinforcements into their V as well.

She checked for pulses. Kerry had none. She checked for Carl's pulse. It was rapid and thready. He was unresponsive. His pupils were fixed and dilated, an ominous sign she knew. She made a decision at that time to send another person back to make sure George was not left at the entrance by himself as it might be his undoing if the killer had backtracked and went down the other V in an attempt to escape. She began to take pictures of the scene as she knew there wasn't anything she could do to change Carl's outcome and it was too late for

Kerry. While she was taking pictures, Greg came upon them with his first aid kit. He had also brought additional lights and reinforcements as well. Hannah was glad of that.

They started setting up more lighting while Greg confirmed her findings. Since they were so far down the cave, he sent one of the crew back to get a backboard to place under Carl if he were to survive. He didn't hold out any hope. If Carl did survive, he would never be much of an asset to the community. He would subsist in one of those care homes being fed, bathed, and turned every two hours until his heart finally gave out. Yet, it wasn't Greg's decision to make. He was only an EMT, not the MD.

It wasn't long before they were able to adequately see what they had stumbled onto. This area was a well equipped video laboratory with a bedroom set with stage lighting on one side of the area, a computer section next to that, and off to the right seemed to be many more pieces of electronics. This was getting deeper and deeper. Hannah continued taking pictures while she insisted everyone start putting on gloves to prevent any more fingerprints being left other than those that had actually been using the equipment. Oh, how she wished for actual power to see what had been being taped. Given the known players thus far, she was afraid this might actually be a child porn site and that upset her tremendously. As she was the head at this site of the cave and Martin was here, he could continue to monitor the progress at this site whilst she continued on with three of the volunteers.

As she moved further into the cave, it was once again getting lighter. Did all of these Vs have upper escapes? This was frightening to know that there were many potential escapes here as well as the possibility of kiddy porn being produced in such a secluded safe spot to not be found.

As they continued, they began to notice they were ascending just like in the other initial V. Hannah was being careful to scan all of the walls, floor, and ceiling for any possible booby traps. She knew that the potential was even greater with the suspected porn being made here. They were almost to the light when she noticed there were spikes up ahead. She stopped the entire team. She needed to look for how these spikes would be set off before letting anyone else get hurt. Her heart fluttered as she noticed where she would next have stepped.

It looked like it might be some type of fossil rock, but she suspected it was the trigger for spikes to be released. She skirted around the fossil rock, being careful not to expose any other risks while looking how the spikes would release, all at one site or multiple sites creating wider damage. It took her another fifteen minutes to ensure that no one would get hurt when she disarmed the spikes. The disarmament took an hour to complete as it was not quite as simple as she had first thought.

Then the team moved forward looking for any signs of bodies, evidence. They were unsuccessful. Yet, once again they were ascending towards the light with the possible same outcome as the previous end light. When they reached it, Hannah ascended to the summit. It was a good thing she didn't have the others ascend with her as they might have served to push her out of the opening and down a 400 foot freefall to the base of the cliff. Not quite the exit as the previous opening. It was something of a surprise as they had found Carl and Kerry had been attacked in this part of the cave.

There weren't any bodies visible at the base of the cliff. There weren't any obvious signs of hiding spots along the way. That meant that they had most likely taken this route and attacked Carl and Kerry and then retraced their steps to take the other V. That meant they should retreat as fast as they could to see how Darrell's team was making out and offer some support along the way.

CHAPTER 31

George was just sitting there as they got back to the juncture. She quickly filled him in on what they had found, what they had done, and what she thought was going on. It was then that the lights came back on. Apparently someone had found the fuse box or repaired the electricity. It certainly made their job a lot easier. However, before Hannah descended down the last V, she made sure her team kept their lights on them to be prepared for any potential power outages.

Hannah hoped that Darrell and his team were okay as well as the other two members of Carl's team that had not shown up as of yet. George hadn't seen anyone from his tunnel come back as of yet. The plan was still to have George sit there and wait to keep an eye on any potential returns of unknown characters or victims.

Thirty minutes later as Hannah and her team made their way down deeper into the mountain; she noticed it was becoming moister and cooler as they progressed without any signs of inhabitants or inhabitation. She hoped they didn't have much longer to go as she was becoming exhausted going in and out of tunnels without any resolution as of yet.

Two hours later they had begun to ascend again without any signs of either team, any known tracks, or other signs of victims or evidence. As they began to ascend, Hannah was glad as it became a little warmer. The only problem with that was that it was now a moist warm and not a dry warm. That was something she would just have to deal with. This day was turning into a long one and she had no idea of time, what time they had started, or how long each of these side trips had taken. She stopped while they all sat for a few minutes, taking a drink of water which they had packed into each of their pockets to ensure they didn't become dehydrated. She tried not to let her frustration show as she knew that if she felt this way, the volunteers must be feeling much the same and would want to desert the effort if frustration got the best of them. She was fortunate as many of them were men and chauvinistic making it less likely that they would allow her to do more or anything better than they did.

It was time though to make a decision of traipsing further or going back for sustenance. There didn't seem to be any sounds up ahead and it was hard telling how much further they would need to go before they found anyone or anything. As she deliberated in her head, she decided it might be best to follow this lead another hour before turning back if no signs of life.

When she rose, the men were fast to do the same as they appeared to want to be that superman or possible next FBI agent. She smiled as she thought of how silly that made them. She wouldn't tell them that though. She needed their numbers, strength, and support and that would end all of that if she said anything. They must have all been somewhat exhilarated by the stop and drinks as they were walking at a slightly faster pace.

They rounded the next corner when they were confronted by the most atrocious site she had ever seen. She tried to keep most of the volunteers from seeing what she had just seen, but was too slow to prevent the majority from initially seeing it which elicited screams of horror which brought the rest right up to the scene right away.

There was Darrel splayed out on the ground with his clothes removed, his arms and legs cut off and moved slightly away from his body. His penis was placed in one of the other dead volunteer's mouth. That volunteer was suspended from the ceiling with what appeared to be lash marks across her body. Her eyes had been removed and her ears were barely hanging on by a thread of tissue.

The other victims were totally unrecognizable. Their scalps and facial dermis had been removed from the back of their heads forward. One had their hands removed, another their feet, and the last had been suspended from the ceiling with their feet tied to their hands with the previous two victims suspended between them. With this gruesome sight, it seemed to be the best idea to backtrack and retrieve a complete law enforcement tactical teams as they would most likely find the other two members of Carl's group in much the same condition and she didn't want to risk any more volunteer's lives pursuing these criminals.

What had started out as a probable arsonist gone wild, was now a psychopathic killer. She needed experts for this hunt, not volunteers. When she suggested they return and get more men for the rest of the search, she didn't get any resistance, even from those previously chauvinistic men. In fact, as they retreated, they were leading the way quite fast with the women volunteers going almost as fast. The good news was that she still didn't hear or see anyone out of the ordinary or clues of where the suspects might be. It still took them three hours to make it back to George and another thirty minutes to make it back to the entrance which didn't appear as any had seen it earlier in the day.

CHAPTER 32

Malcolm, George, and Hannah sat down to eat while they discussed what they had thus far. George did the honor of bringing Hannah up to date with his and Carl's actual investigation, the crime board which Malcolm had retrieved, and his suspicions that it was most likely Jasper who had been the culprit before finding Darrell's and his team's bodies in that condition. Malcolm brought them up to date with what they had found in the outer room which they were sitting amongst as they ate as well as the taping that had been occurring in the inner taping room. It seemed that Jessie and Janice were avid porn stars as evidenced by the majority of the tapes. It appeared that they had initiated Jasper into the life first as his tapes seemed to start at a much younger age than what Catherine's tapes began. There wasn't any tapes with Julia, Gantry, or Stanford even mentioned or seen.

Thus far, they had a correlation between Jasper, Catherine, Jessie, and Janice. There was also a correlation between Jasper, Catherine, Julia, Stanford, Jessie, and Janice as family and friends at least known to the neighbors. How did Gantry fit into this? He didn't have any past history of kidnapping or porn, just arson. So, was he someone they had found that new how to create an explosion? If so, how had they found him?

It was at that time that Malcolm received a communication via his phone that stated the dead man beneath the debris was Jessie Brooks AKA Jessie the Rat who had grown up in the same area as Gantry had. Now they were getting some correlations. However, that didn't explain why Jessie was dead beneath the rubble, why Janice wasn't nearby as well, nor who was left and killing everyone within the cave. Malcolm had sent a search team up to examine the well worn trail from the first cave opening they had discovered but hadn't heard back from them.

Hannah shared that she felt like they had probably walked a good five miles descending and then ascending with the direction she would have to assume was actually towards the center of the mountain. When they had found the bodies, they still didn't seem to visualize any lights or smell fresh air. She then asked the obvious question, "Who turned on all of the lights?"

"Not me!" George and Malcolm said together. Now they all looked at one another with consternation. This was not a good sign. Since none of them including Malcolm's team had turned on the lights, they were either on a timer, or the lights had been turned on further into the cave than Hannah had investigated. That meant there was obviously another way into the cave and they had essentially wasted all day and five dead people while the perpetrators were most likely gone.

Malcolm was immediately on the phone in contact with the team who were supposed to be following the trail from the first opening. They had been walking for hours without finding any clues other than this trail seemed to be used almost daily by many persons. He asked them to continue until they were not able to see anymore then camp for the night. What a stupid request as the leader of that search group informed him the sun had set two hours ago and they were getting ready to get some sleep and start again in the morning.

Malcolm got up, walked to the entrance to the cave to confirm that it was indeed night time. He looked at his watch. It was nearing midnight. He made another phone call asking for a night search to be conducted by the flight team to see if they could isolated any heat sources other than the known search team on the trail. He asked that a map of all known trails be sent to his laptop ASAP as well. He then requested that they contact the Indian Reservation in the morning to see if anyone knew of any hidden caves along this mountain and would be able or willing to assist with the search.

With those phone calls made, Malcolm updated Hannah and George and suggested they get some sleep before starting early in the morning.

CHAPTER 33

Four a.m. came early. Yet, Malcolm really wanted to get an early start. He sent a team of crime scene investigators into the Brooks home to dust for prints as well as look for any additional evidence linking them to the porn as well as the other members of these crimes. Hannah and George were still sleeping. He took this opportunity to take his laptop to the exterior of the mountain and access the internet to see what additional information he could find to hopefully help wrap up this investigation before any more lives were lost.

He was deep into his internet work, when Hannah brought over a cup of coffee for him to drink. He looked up at her and saw the look of exhaustion on her face. He knew she must not have slept good last night as her eyes had larger bags beneath them this morning than they had last night before they attempted to sleep. They were trying to discuss the case quietly as not to wake George who had been working this case the longest and had lost the most thus far. They wondered if he was aware of his recent promotion via his supervisor's death. They weren't about to add that level of distress to his already worried mind. They needed his brain as he seemed to actually have the earliest handle of who might have been responsible even before the FBI agents had.

They had decided that they had enough information to put out an APB on Gantry, Jasper, Julia, Janice, and Catherine as armed and dangerous, to approach with caution after calling for backup. They then updated Carl's crime scene board with their recent pieces of information including Janice's prints matching a teenage runaway from Iowa by the name of Alysson Cartz. Now, they were beginning to get an idea of what had been going on. Gantry and Jessie had grown up near one another. Gantry had been present for Twin Towers explosions. He had been suspected of a bombing incident in the town near where Alysson had grown up. Jessie and Alysson had produced years of porn. Jasper had starred in some of their child porn as had Catherine. Gantry must have been traveling with Jessie during some of these escapades. Jasper must have met Gantry and learned some techniques from them or Stanford had met Gantry somehow to perform the first explosion. Yet, Stanford may or may not have been aware of the relationship between Jessie and Gantry and Jasper or he would not have planned the death of Jasper, Julia, or Catherine. Or Stanford may not have been aware of the original explosion as he may have been the set fall guy for the explosion. Yet, he had been killed in an explosion at the Brooks garage. That must have been unsettling for them to have their home searched for evidence or they had already planned their departure to another place when it occurred. It was unfortunate that

Stanford had expired as he would have most likely become the fall guy for the original explosion. If they had simply stopped at the first explosion, they would not have triggered this much involvement from the FBI. In fact, there probably would not have been more investigation past the original fire if they had not set the next explosion of the truck or terminated Stanford's life. Someone must have been really mad at Stanford to have exploded his truck, and then taken his life in the garage. Was it Julia? Did Alysson have a secret relationship with Stanford? Had Jasper or Catherine really hated their father that much? Was Gantry getting rid of the male competition he had amongst this crowd?

Each of these questions was concerning. They couldn't afford to narrow the possibility to only one scenario and miss out on the real situation. Yet, they did need to expedite the process as well as get a resolution as fast as possible. Malcolm decided to find any additional information about the relationship between Alysson and Gantry, if there had been any relationship between Julia, Alysson, and / or Gantry. While he would be performing that, Hannah and George were taking a task force to retrieve the dead bodies and continue to search for the perpetrators. They would enlist Candi as a point person for the trails investigation. Candi was ecstatic to finally be a more integral part of the investigative team. Her enthusiasm would be helpful with the tediousness of coordinating a team of investigators checking each of the trails.

That being said, they started their day in earnest.

CHAPTER 34

Malcolm immediately started his internet search of crimes committed by Gantry to see if anyone matching Alysson's description could be found as a possible perpetrator or contact. While his computer was working on that search, he spent time on the phone with Mayo Clinic to evaluate the possibility of a relationship between Julia and Alysson or Gantry. That was a bust. No luck. He then retraced some of George's steps with his investigation of Jasper's treatment.

That did retrieve some additional information that George was not given. Just the mention of FBI and the flood gates opened. Jasper and Gantry had forged a very close relationship while he was in his treatment. In fact, they shared that they had let Gantry go as they suspected the relationship between Jasper and Gantry may not have been healthy or one that they wanted to be responsible for. Shortly after firing Gantry, Jasper had left the treatment facility with a much more reserved and reticent attitude. They of course reiterated that if they had known Gantry was who he was; they wouldn't have hired him nor allowed him to be anywhere near young boys.

Now, that was a good piece of information and explained how Gantry, Alysson, and Jasper were connected, or at least partially. There was the question of whether Jasper was sexually promiscuous prior to his treatment, initiated during, or after the treatment. Malcolm doubted that the treatment facility was responsible for Jasper's sexual desires since he had seen many tapes of Jasper's scenes which appeared to be voluntary throughout the collection that he had viewed. Given the tapes found, Jasper probably had known and participated in the filming prior to his treatment. It may have been the real reason for his behavioral change and no one had been perceptive enough to see what had been occurring.

If Jasper had been performing in these films for the last five years as it seemed when comparing the dates upon the tapes that meant he had known Alysson for at least five years. Whether or not he had known Gantry that long it was unclear. It was evident that Alysson had known Gantry much longer than that. Upon further research, Julia had known Gantry and Alysson for longer than five years. He stumbled upon this little tidbit of information when he had looked back at one of the tapes older than five years. There was an acknowledgement for Julia's professional contribution for professional consultation. The name of the film, "A New Kind of Therapy," left little to the imagination when it was viewed. Malcolm quit reviewing the tape after the first five minutes of film. Was Julia responsible for encouraging of exploiting her own son's sexual curiosity for profit?

Judging from the date on Julia's contribution film and the dates when Jasper had started performing, it appeared that she may have been an instigator or at least aware that it was occurring. Given this piece of information, it didn't necessarily explain why Jasper or Gantry may have spared Julia from the original explosion or fire. Julia must have a strong relationship with Gantry as well, or was it with Alysson?

With these thoughts swirling in his head, he hoped that Hannah and George were having more luck than he had.

Chapter 35

Hannah and George were not enthusiastic about their initial need to retrieve the dead bodies, but three hours later, they had sent the five dead bodies back with the forensic investigator and his team. Now, they were once again in the dark. The lights had gone off. That meant they would need to be careful with their ongoing exploration so there were no more injuries or deaths. Four hours later, they felt exhausted and like a failure.

When Hannah looked down at her pedometer, they had searched approximately four miles without any more Vs, no signs of light, and no sense of walking up or down, just horizontally level. Given the potential that if the perpetrators had also retracted their steps and had exited via one of the other exits, the search of this cave might be for naught. They decided to take a snack break and sat down for thirty minutes while reviewing the potential situations.

The break was what they needed to realize that if the perpetrators had retraced their steps and exited via one of the holes, then Candi's teams would find them on the outer surface of the mountain. Thus, what they were doing was essential to not allowing them to escape via this outlet. They started searching once again with the intention to stop for a break in five hours.

They had probably gone about another forty-five feet when Hannah noticed what looked like another trip wire. She halted the team. Brought all the lights to where she was to get a better view of the possible trip wire. It was definitely there. The question was where the beginning and end of the trip wire was, what it would trigger. It actually invigorated the team as they assumed that meant the perpetrators must be further in and afraid that the investigators were not giving up easily.

Hannah and Russell quietly looked for the beginning of the trip wire to the left of the group. George and Hank looked to the right. Each was being extremely careful not to accidentally release the wire and whatever it would unleash. Thirty minutes later, George announced they had found it holding a small explosive charge which Hank was attempting to disarm. He encouraged the remaining team to retreat to where they had taken their break. Hannah had found that their end was simply secured tightly into the wall of the cave. Both she and Russell retreated along with George back to the area that they had taken a break. It was only a few more minutes when Hank shouted "all clear" and waited for the team to come back to him.

Once there, they were ready to continue their investigation. They now noticed that they seemed to be climbing at a rather rapid rate. It almost seemed like they were actually elevating a foot with every step. They proceeded at this pace and rapid ascension for another mile when they noticed it seemed to be getter lighter instead of steeped in total darkness. Hannah asked everyone to remain quiet and turn their lights off to see what or where this avenue of light might be coming from. Everyone was quick to obey. They didn't see any direct light sources, couldn't hear anything ahead, but decided it was time to be careful and essentially quiet as they progressed further.

They turned their lamps back on and progressed in silence towards the dim light. There were more markings along the cave wall. They weren't sure exactly what they were, but they weren't going to take the time to decipher them either. They had ascended approximately another mile when the light was much brighter with the sound of running water. They hoped it was running outside of the cave or they were going to be washed away like rodents in the middle of a flood.

They turned off all but one light. That light was used to make sure there were no booby traps. They walked slowly for the next half mile. Now, they could smell the fresh air, hear the running water, and wondered where they were exactly. They didn't see or hear anything like the perpetrators or what might be misconstrued as potential attacks. They were slowing on the ascent and seemed to be walking almost horizontal once again as the walked the next half mile. This journey was rapidly coming to an end as they walked into a nice alcove behind a large waterfall. It made for a beautiful scene.

Hannah had to give them credit. No one would have found this entrance if not for the cave finally leading to this exit. She was going to be careful while she and George searched the edges of the waterfall to see if there was a ledge or path to follow out of here.

It didn't take long before both found pathways exiting on each side of the waterfall. There were ten of them which they split into two teams of five to search the paths. They would need to get a safe distance from the waterfall before attempting to contact Candi and Malcolm as they would never be able to hear them or be heard. They made a pact to call the other team within the next thirty minutes to check on where they were and to not let anyone get hurt.

CHAPTER 36

I t didn't take George long to ask if anyone needed to use the facilities, take a break, or have something to eat while he tried to contact Candi. Everyone wanted to progress, but also realized the need to see if Candi or Malcolm had found anything while they had been busy in the cave. They also realized they had no supplies for the night which was rapidly approaching and could use a little drop of some tents, food, etc. Thus, they all agreed to take a short break while George tried his phone call.

George was unable to get thru to Candi, but had left a message on her cell, the work phone, her home phone to triangulate his position off his cell and drop them some supplies as soon as she received his messages. He then tried to reach Malcolm to update him on where they were and whether they had found anything new at his end.

Once again, George had been unsuccessful. Once again he had left messages asking for nighttime supplies. Then he tried Hannah. He was able to get through to her cell phone. Finally, success. He was glad to find out that she had already spoken to Candi and Malcolm, got an update on what they had found out so far, as well as asking they send in supplies for the night. She quickly updated George on Malcolm's minimal findings, Candi's lack of finding anyone as of yet, and the proposed use of night flights over the mountain looking for potential perpetrators outside of where Hannah and his teams were located.

They were all bedding down for the night after performing a little hand fishing back at the waterfall while waiting on the tents and other supplies. After receiving the supplies, they had rapidly erected the tents and proceeded to bed down for the night.

CHAPTER 37

It was all of four o'clock when they got up the next morning. They made quick work of eating and breaking down the tents. Then they proceeded to start back along the trail to see if they could find something that was missed on the unsuccessful night flights.

They had been trudging along for an hour when the trail suddenly widened into a beautiful clearing. The surprising thing about this clearing is that the area seemed to be used. He stopped everyone before the area could be contaminated with their own stuff. Then he asked who might be familiar with tracks, other signs of use as the clearing seemed to be well used. Samantha came forward and suggested she could interpret some of the signs. She pulled out her trusty camera, started taking pictures, and examining different tracks, broken twigs, etc. Everyone waited with baited breath hoping that she would tell them they had found the right trail.

She was still working the clearing an hour later and the rest of the team were getting restless. She had been silent during the entire time she had been working which was frustrating to the rest of the team. George asked her what she had found thus far. She didn't answer right away which only seemed to bait the team's frustration even more.

"Well.........at first I thought it was a bust as most of the tracks at the far entry where you are ....seem to be animals of different sorts..................................... but then it gets interesting............as you near the center and the area where I am currently........." She stopped what she was doing and just stood there.

George was immediately concerned. "What is it?"

"I am going to need some help. There are a couple of half eaten bodies over here."

"STOP! Which of you are actual crime scene investigators?"

"I am!" The other three answered together.

"Samantha is there any areas which you need us to avoid as we come towards you to investigate the bodies?"

"Try to come to the right as you come towards me as I need to continue looking to the right to see what I might find besides this mess."

The team proceeded towards her carefully staying to the right while trying not to let their anticipation at finding some dead bodies. However, when they neared there, they didn't find easily identifiable bodies. Instead, initially it looked like they were two smaller frame people or children simply by the size of the proposed bodies. One appeared as if it might be female and the other like it was male. They split into two teams of two. One team taking the female body and the other the male. Samantha continued her search of other signs.

Each team took out their cameras and documented the site. Upon close up range, it became evident that the two bodies were actually tied to one another. This had been no accident. It was a planned detour that the investigators would have to take. George took that moment to call Malcolm and ask for additional help looking in his direction. Malcolm was quick to offer additional help stating the cave was no longer an essential part of the picture. He would send half of his remaining team to George's site and the other half to Hannah. He stated he would coordinate with Candi back at headquarters where he would have more consistent internet to support the field operations. He asked if one of the investigators could set up their cell phone to take the prints and send them to him for identification. He wanted to make sure this was not another set of innocent bystanders versus Catherine and Jasper or Gantry and Julia or Janice.

Carson had been busy obtaining what he could of any identifiable prints and had sent them to Malcolm while George had been talking to him. It also allowed Malcolm to give exact coordinates to the pilot to drop the support team. Now they were all working in quiet as they examined their bodies for any potential evidence or possible identification.

An hour later their support team arrived. They had news. The victims were not any of the known perpetrators. They were two teenagers who were believed to have been abducted from two different neighboring communities. They had been residents at the same treatment facility where Jasper had been at also at the same time as both he and Gantry had been there. This added another dimension to the puzzle. Had they been abducted or participated willingly? Or had they been like Alysson? Initially, a runaway and then abducted? Had they been the unnamed newest additions to the kiddie porn? They had found evidence of the two kids being tied together in such a fashion to be bait for any wandering carnivore searching for food. It even appeared that there might have been an initial cut on one or both of them to entice carnivorous animals to attack them and possibly remove all evidence prior to the team finding them. Based upon body temperature of both it was difficult to determine how long they had been out here as it had been both warm and cold. However, based upon the fact that they were tied to one another, they had the explosion at the cave a little over four days ago and the group probably had at least a day's head start on them. That being said, the team now had gained some of their momentum as they had found a clue that meant they were likely on the track of these individuals and not chasing a golden goose.

George, Samantha, and three of the newest additions from Malcolm's team decided to forge ahead looking for additional clues while the others finished investigating this site and sending the bodies back for further investigation and then joined George's group. They now wanted to hurry but knew the potential hazards of moving too quickly from the deaths of their fallen peers in the cave. They maintained there diligence hoping to find additional clues and maintain safety for themselves and the remainder of the team as they rejoined them.

They had been walking level for so long that they noticed they were beginning to get a little winded as they were going along now. With that observation, George decided to look around and noticed that even though it had appeared they were walking level, he was able to peer through and down an opening in the trees to see the waterfall which they had camped near the night before. They must be climbing in elevation. That meant the perpetrators would also be feeling the effects of the climb. He looked around for any clues of using a possible cane or walking stick to make it easier to do. He was successful at spotting a somewhat heavy marking along the right of the trail. He stopped the team to see if he could identify when those marks had been made. Samantha was unable to determine how old the impressions were. They moved forward once again.

They had been moving forward for another thirty minutes when Samantha asked if they could stop for a break to eat and become accustomed to the altitude. George was agreeable. He was accustomed to changing altitudes more frequently than the rest of the team apparently, but he was hungry also. They found a clearing about another fifty feet where they could sit down comfortably and eat. They did so. They continued to wait upon the other portion of the team and take a little break while they did so. They only waited about another thirty minutes for the remaining team. The other team asked to be allowed to eat and accustom themselves as well. George's team was agreeable so they discussed what the other team had found after they had departed while they ate. They had found some signs of torture of the two teens. They had had multiple small stabbings in their backs and thighs and then had been placed in such a manner to make it difficult for carnivorous animals to get to those stab sites. They had been left alive with minor wounds for the animals to find. It must have been terrifying for them. That brought up the question that if they were only one day behind, how they had missed the screams when they had been found by the carnivorous animals. That must mean they were more than one day and likely at least two days behind the perpetrators.

George called Malcolm with their preliminary findings and asked if Hannah had found anything on her trail that would encourage her to continue or if they should send search planes out in angles from where they were located now. Malcolm said he hadn't heard from Hannah in the last eight hours and needed to check on her progress as well as sending out the search planes.

They decided not to wait to see if Hannah and her group could meet up with them before progressing. They gathered their trash and started down the trail once again. Only this time, they seemed to be going at a slight decline as opposed to going uphill. They were actually beginning to go down a much steeper trail which seemed to be riding along the edge of a cliff. They slowed tremendously to prevent any big mishaps or possibility of any booby traps that were difficult to spot becoming a problem.

They had been walking for another three hours at that slow pace on a steep incline before they noticed a leveling and direction away from the cliff. They began to relax their guard somewhat as they were more comfortable not being at the edge of a cliff. George tried to remain ever diligent and alert while leading back towards the forestation. He happened to look up and notice that the sun was setting so he decided that they needed to make camp at the next available campsite. That took about another fifteen minutes of trekking before they came to a nice clearing. George let Samantha check it out before allowing the others to set up tents.

Then, while the team were setting up the tents and cooking their evening meal, he once again checked in with Malcolm to see what Hannah had found or if there was something else they needed to do. Malcolm was concerned as he had not heard anything from Hannah's team yet. He was sending a search party and plane to see if there were any signs of where they were. If he didn't get any clues by morning, he was afraid he would have to consider her team another casualty of the search which really concerned him.

This being said, he encouraged George to let his team go ahead and enjoy the evening as he needed them to pick up the pace early in the am.

CHAPTER 38

George was glad to have had the break last night. He had slept so solid that he had not even heard the circling search planes. His first phone call was to Malcolm who let him know that there had been significant findings on the trail Hannah had followed. The search flights had not found any sighting of Hannah or her team so they had dropped some paratroopers who started investigating the trail. They had found a recent explosion at the opening to a cave a mere twenty minutes past Malcolm's last communication with Hannah. They had been working at removing rubble by hand all night with minimal impact on the debris. However, they did hear an SOS when they had first started letting them know someone was still alive. They were still at it this morning with fresh recruit arriving to help out as they spoke. They had confirmed that the trapped individuals were all still alive and seemed to be having no problems with oxygen deprivation. They had chosen not to investigate further as they didn't think it wise to progress past their current spot without sufficient assistance or an avenue of escape from the perpetrators. George was glad to learn that they seemed to be okay despite being trapped within a cave. He clarified with Malcolm that they were to continue their trail investigation. Malcolm was adamant that he wanted to leave no stones unturned and wanted to find these bandits as soon as they could. He didn't want to end the third week of this investigation without resolution even if it meant a twenty-four hour operation from now on.

George understood that mentality as he was feeling the stress as well. He pulled his team together and quickly updated them while breaking down the camp. They were ready to push forward as fast as was safe. They reminded George it was not necessarily safe to move too quickly and end up at the end of a rock slide or explosion like had been done multiple times already by these perpetrators. That being shared, they moved out. They had been on the trail for an hour when they came upon another cave at the end of the trail. Before entering the cave, George called Malcolm to let him know they were getting ready to enter a cave to investigate. He asked Malcolm to check with one of the local Indian reservations to see if anyone was aware of this connecting with the area that had collapsed past Hannah's team. Malcolm was glad to know that they had found this cave opening and would follow up with one of the local reservation trail experts.

George and his team entered after checking for any exterior or interior triggers for a rock slide or explosion. They were glad to find none. They all turned on their lanterns as it was almost immediately dark. They traipsed along for six hours, going up, then down, then up again. Then they found a huge clearing with natural light entering from above and a small pool with clear water and small fish swimming around. Thank goodness they hadn't found any snakes or bears within the cave, nor any signs of any. They took a break and ate in quiet wondering what they would find after this area. Samantha had wandered slightly away when they heard a loud rumble from the direction of the opening to the cave through which they had entered.

"CRAP!" George scrambled to see what they might be able to do. However, he thought he might try using the cell phone to check on Malcolm's progress. Hopefully the signal would exit through the opening at the ceiling of the cave.

"Malcolm! Malcolm! Can you hear me?"

"You don't have to shout. I can hear you just fine. What's the problem?"

"We're trapped in the cave. We just heard a rumble from the direction of the opening. We were finally taking a break in the first clearing within the cave when we heard it. The only good thing about this is there is this opening at the ceiling that is allowing the signal to exit. Would you like to set a team down above us to at least lower a rope ladder that we could use to exit with if unable to find another opening?"

"That's interesting. Hold on for another minute while I get the coordinates and I will send a team out to put a rope ladder down as well as guard the opening to make sure someone else doesn't use it to escape. You will be interested in knowing that you are less than a half mile away from Hannah's team according to your coordinates. It might be interesting if you investigate further into the cave and find Hannah from the inside. Then we would know how they were able to trap and hurt both of you at the same time."

"OK. I am going to put you on speaker so the rest of the members can hear what you said."

Malcolm reiterated on the speaker phone. Then they all broke the camp and started walking once again. They had been walking for thirty minutes when they found the path veered in two directions. They stopped to discuss whether they would split into two groups and investigate each or investigate one and then the other. They decided to do the second choice using the veering to the right as it seemed like it would be the most likely to lead them to Hannah.

They were walking for another hour when they heard what sounded like rocks pounding upon themselves. They took a minute to take it in. Then they continued on. As they neared the pounding rocks, they began to hear voices. They slowed as not to come upon the perpetrators instead of Hannah's crew. They were looking up, down, around, to make sure there were no more booby traps. As they looked around, the voices sounded as if they were getting closer to them. They decided they would separate to both sides of the cave and wait to make sure it was Hannah's team before announcing themselves.

It seemed like eons as they waited for the voices to get closer. They still sounded like they were some distance away. That made it extremely difficult to keep quiet and not give away their location. George could see the others were as fidgety as he was, but they all maintained their silence.

"I wonder how far before we run into George's team?"

"We're right here."

Then they heard running down the cave towards them. George's team stayed in place hoping against hope that Hannah's team didn't trigger another booby trap. Luck was with them thus far, no sounds of a cave in and here they were. They quickly progressed back to the open clearing with the rope ladder access to freedom. It didn't seem to take as long as the trek to find Hannah's team.

When they reached the clearing, Hannah's team exited into sunlight as they needed that reality that they were living and no longer trapped in the cave. Malcolm sent a new team in to assist George with investigating the other avenue of the veering. They immediately started off with the investigation of the second veering. They didn't have long to investigate it as it opened into another clearing which had a small opening with light slightly visible on the other side of the opening. They neared it carefully wondering if it was also booby trapped or part of a rock slide to cover tracks. When they were on top of it, it appeared that the opening was purposeful. The wall seemed to have been constructed from the other side and the opening a reminder of where to start or what was on the other side.

That being said, they started slowly removing rocks at the top to the side. They were careful to check each for any sign of a trip wire or booby trap. They were not having any difficulty removing the wall. It was meant to be a temporary fixture so that it could be torn down and rebuilt as needed. They had been at the breakdown of the wall for four hours before they had a clear vision of what was on the other side. It was at the edge of a ravine. They needed to be extremely careful so that they didn't end up falling over the edge as they continued to clear rocks.

George tried calling Malcolm to update him. He didn't get through; the cell service was not working. Mark was one of the new members who stepped forward. "I have a walkie talkie that we could try."

George was willing to give it a try. It was successful. That was good news. Malcolm was glad to know they had found a new opening and he quickly grabbed the coordinates. He informed them that new recruits would be there shortly via helicopter flight. George was happy but overwhelmed as he realized this was becoming a drawn out investigation without resolution as of yet. When he turned back to the wall to see what the other's progress with tearing it down was, he was amazed to see that it was almost all gone.

Yet, he couldn't help but have a little trepidation as he neared the wall. The others were no longer removing any of the rocks, nor were they talking. They were standing still and staring all in the same general direction. Given the past findings along the trail, George was afraid he was going to see more gruesome bodies.

He was not disappointed. There were three bodies hanging upside down in a tree burned to a crisp. George immediately tried to call Malcolm on the cell phone. He was so upset; he had forgotten there was no service available. He then grabbed the walkie talkie and proceeded to let Malcolm know that they needed to send additional body bags, etc.

His team decided to wait for reinforcements before approaching the bodies. They had been sitting there in complete silence when they heard the whoop, whoop sound of the helicopter propellers and gunshots. Why would they hear gun shots? Each of them made a grab for their own holsters in response to the gunshots.

Now, it once again seemed like an eternity. The sun was going down. Lighting was becoming more difficult to make out different items without lighting a fire or their lanterns. How were they supposed to know if the helicopter that hadn't made it yet was theirs or if they were going to be expecting the shooters coming their way?

George took a chance and made another attempt at communicating with Malcolm via the walkie talkie. It was unsuccessful. He tried his cell phone knowing that would be unsuccessful as well. He had to try. It appeared they were on their own. He told everyone it would be best if they actually went back into the cave to be out of easy vision or easy targets for anyone just incase they were the perpetrators instead of Malcolm's new recruits. They appeared to be happy to let George call the shots and quickly reentered the cave. They provided a small fire behind a new wall they erected with the rocks that had been torn down earlier. They then sat down to eat something while waiting.

They were waiting, waiting, waiting. George could not allow all of them to sleep at the same time with the risk of being attacked while sleeping so he set up shifts of two for two hours each to watch for any potential hazards.

CHAPTER 39

They had been vigilant all night without any occurrences. George tried the walkie talkie this morning without any luck. He tried his cell phone without any luck as well. That being said, he decided it was up to him to call the shots as he would as the temporary sheriff. He announced that they would take pictures in the good light of the scene outside and then proceed to follow the trail and the perpetrators who probably only numbered two if these three bodies were possibly any combination of the Schotts, Alysson or Gantry.

Everyone agreed with his plan other than Samantha. She insisted that they proceed without her as she would document the site while waiting on the recruits to let them know where the rest of the team had progressed to. George didn't think it was the safest plan to leave Samantha by herself and asked if anyone would volunteer to stay with her. Mark was very enthusiastic about staying with Samantha. George wondered if Mark thought he might influence Samantha or if he was not all that an enthusiastic investigator. George insisted upon Mark and Samantha keeping the walkie talkie so that if Malcolm came back in range they could also let him know what they had decided to do as well as never seeing the helicopter and extra help.

George and his crew started off at a fast clip but soon found that to be exhausting as they had begun to climb in altitude. They slowed. They were always close to the edge of the cliffs as they walked without any hint of coverage if someone had a clear vision. This was not too much of a concern as they were not able to easily seen over the edge and had a false sense of security that meant others could not see them easily as well.

Four hours later they came upon a zip line. They took a few minutes to discuss the option of using the zip line, being at the perpetrators' mercy if they were waiting on the other end of the line, if they had even taken the zip line, and if they didn't take the zip line, what was the likelihood that they would end up at the same spot as the perpetrators? They spent more and more time discussing these options. In fact, they were not coming to a consensus. Given this, George took a chance and called Malcolm. It went through. Malcolm thought it best that two members were allowed to use the zip line with the second strapping an okay sign on the sip to promote the rest of the team coming down the zip line. Malcolm marked George's coordinates to be aware of where the team was at the present. After speaking with Malcolm, the team was ready for two to take that chance. Glory and Jeffrey set off on their zip ride. The other members sit there waiting. It seemed like an eternity before they received word it was okay to take the zip line ride.

Prior to taking the zip line himself, George made one last phone call to Malcolm asking what the headways were with all other teams, any potential sightings from the air, and what the next plan was. Malcolm could only tell George that the three bodies had been unofficially identified as Alysson, Julia, and Gantry strictly based on the sizes of the corpses. He stressed, however, that that was not a guarantee and to not that allow him to be too cocky while pursuing Jasper and Catherine as it may not turn out that was who the corpses were. George promised that once he was at the end of the zip line, he would continue to proceed with caution, but hope that this crazy chase would soon end and with no more casualties if possible.

George organized everyone once again at the bottom of the zip line after quickly updating them on the status and Malcolm's intuition as far as who the three bodies had been. They started off on the path once again. They hadn't gone far when they found a nice pool of water at the base of a waterfall. Glory begged for the opportunity to take a quick swim to cool off. The others were not the least hesitant as they hadn't bathed in over a week and it was hot. They didn't skinny dip, but Glory's clothing choices left no room for imagination once wet. Yet, no one seemed to be paying any attention. The water was that enticing. They frolicked for a little longer and as George was getting ready to call it quits, he decided to look behind the water to check for any potential cave as they may miss this clue like they almost did before.

It was a good thing he checked. It was not only a cave, but a well stocked, well sheltered, well equipped cave. He called to the others to come see what he had found. They didn't come at once. He called again. No answer. He was getting ready to go outside the cave when he heard talking. He listened. This was not any of the members of his group.

These voices sounded young. They were discussing what to do with his other team mates. They were asking one another whether they should hang and fry them like before, whether they should stake them out over an ant hill to be slowly eaten alive, or whether they should find some really heavy rocks and tie it to them to help them sink. The good news about this is they didn't seem to know that he was part of the group who was not part of the group. However, he didn't have any type of weapon to take on at least these two younger perpetrators. He needed to think of what to do and with what while they deliberated about what they would do with his investigators.

He certainly couldn't hope to surprise them as his wet clothes would make too much noise. If he attacked them naked, he would still need some type of weapon. What he needed to do was take a peek to see if he could get a better idea of what was there, where it was, what his best opportunity of surprise would be. Immediately upon raising himself up to look, he noticed that it was both Jasper and Catherine holding his investigators at gun point with their hands and mouths duct taped. They were now arguing about the best course to get rid of them. They were all very close over at the other side of the cave without any potential areas to hide behind and attack from on this side of the cave.

While he was debating his options, something surprising happened. Jasper and Catherine's arguing stopped with their heated kissing. They seemed to be oblivious of everyone's watching with disgust. This had to be his only opportunity to attack-when they were preoccupied with themselves and their sex. He quickly and as quietly as he could got out of the water. He tried to rush over as quickly as he could to grab one of the guns. Just as he had grabbed the gun that Jasper had dropped during the sex, Catherine noticed him over Jasper's shoulder. She tried to grab her gun to shoot him. His reflex was protection. He let off three shots into Jasper which must have also entered Catherine's body as she jerked back as they seemed to enter Jasper's body. Then they were both went limp. He couldn't seem to move. Wasn't he supposed to check them? To see if they were dead? Shouldn't he let the others out of their duct tape? Shouldn't he check to see if there were any others who might be able to attack?

Then, his attention was drawn to the other investigators who were trying to get his attention. They were all trying to get him to look behind him. He was not sure he wanted to look behind him as he felt the hairs on the back of his neck stand on end. He stood rooted to the spot for a second more which felt like minutes. Then he bent and rolled to his right shooting at a spot which had been right behind him. When he looked at that spot now, he was surprised to see what he had shot. There was a giant brown bear laying dead.

He didn't take much time now, starting to cut the duct tape off of the other investigators. They also didn't take much time to remove the remaining duct tape form their wrists and mouths. They quickly took in what had happened. They spent mere seconds organizing themselves to look for any additional clues or other potential perpetrators and evidence. They suggested that George go outside and try to contact Malcolm to let him know they thought they were done with the investigation and had managed to finish off the remaining perpetrators.

George did as they suggested only to be informed that they may have found Jasper and Catherine, but that they still didn't have any remains matching Julia or Gantry. If they didn't find any clues for where they had gone, he would have to call it quits on the investigation for the time being. George was having some difficulty dealing with his adrenaline rush let down so he decided to just sit for a time while he tried to process all of the information before letting the others in on what he knew now.

CHAPTER 40

He was unsure how long he had been sitting there before Jeffrey came out to see what he had found out. He felt so exhausted that he had to take several breaths while relating what Malcolm had told him. He then asked Jeffrey what they had discovered inside thus far. Jeffrey enlightened him over a bottle of water they had found when searching. While Jeffrey was relaying the information, he began coughing. Suddenly, he was on the ground grasping his throat. Quickly, George pulled out his knife and slit a hole in Jeffrey's throat where he was able to breathe through. He immediately called for help. No one answered or came. He left Jeffrey to see what the others were doing that they didn't hear him or why they didn't respond. He was very mad and almost rushed in, but stopped just short of rushing in. Gantry and Julia had not been found and the others might be hostage once again.

He slowed as he neared the entrance, listening for any sounds. There were none. He pulled the gun out of his back waistband. He approached with caution. He peeked around the corner to see what was going on. He found all of the others on the ground not breathing. He didn't see anyone else. He rushed back to Jeffrey. He immediately started a fire to sear the emergency tracheotomy and stop the bleeding. Once he completed that, he put Malcolm on speaker phone while he updated him on what he had found, suspected poisoning of the bottled water, and would not try to save any of the others, nor would he try to investigate anything additional without additional help and an air ambulance to lift Jeffrey out for better emergency intervention.

All he heard was Malcolm swearing while he heard background typing on computer keys. Then his conversation with Malcolm was drown out by the helicopter overhead. Emergency personnel were coming down the ropes to help Jeffrey and assess the others for possible signs of life or cause of death. All George could do was to sit still holding his head in his hands.

"George…."

George looked up to see Malcolm standing there. He was just standing there looking down at George, not sure what he should say, nor how he should say it to make things less traumatic than they were. Instead, he just placed a hand on George's shoulder for comfort. That seemed the least that he could do. Then he joined the rest of the investigative team inside of the cave to see what they could find to help complete the search or to finalize the lack of evidence.

Malcolm spent the next five hours inside of the cave with the investigative team searching for any and all possible avenues of escape, clues to the whereabouts of Julia or Gantry, whether the water had been poisoned or something on the surface of what was searched was deadly. What was found was the surface was tainted with a large amount of curare which was undetectable to the naked eye. The question was how Jeffrey managed to survive when all the rest had not. That would have to be something to ask him later when he was alert. The other significant clues were that there was some more computer equipment which was initially hidden within stacks of bottled water. The initial investigation of the computer demonstrated recent internet searches of different destination sites. Upon a little more in depth review of the computer, Malcolm was able to find a recent printing of tickets to the Bahamas leaving from Phoenix in a matter of minutes. With that piece of information, he called the airlines asking for an immediate delay in the takeoff while staying on the flight line. Then he made the next phone call to the local police asking them to remove Gantry and Julia from the flight and hold them at headquarters until they were able to arrive for final questioning. With that, he left the majority of the team to finish the site investigation and took George with him.

CHAPTER 41

When they arrived at the Phoenix police station, they were met with a multitude of media personnel who had somehow found out about the arrest of Julia and Gantry. Malcolm was able to easily avoid them and George was still dealing with a little shock so he was simply walking somewhat like a zombie behind Malcolm. When they made it inside, the chief of police was there to greet them. He wanted to make a statement about who they had arrested, why, and how they had worked together to nab these killers. Malcolm let him have his say and then stated they would remove the prisoners to a FBI site. He had brought his officers to do just that. He allowed the chief of police to make his statement while his officers took the pair out the back door to the FBI offices.

Upon arrival at the FBI facility, the pair knew they were in some trouble that would be more difficult to escape.

While at the local police station, they were likely to have been arraigned quickly and released on their own recognizance or on bail. Here, that option was highly improbable. They were separated upon arrival. Each asked for a lawyer, both had been told, the attorney would arrive when the FBI allowed them to enter the facility. If a lawyer had been contacted prior to their removal from Phoenix police station, they were unlikely to find them as there was no record of their removal or to where they might be. Malcolm had made certain of that by not allowing the chief of police or anyone else be aware of where they would be taking them.

Malcolm started with Julia as she was the newest at this and most likely to crack in his opinion. She was just sitting there tapping her fingers as if impatient. Malcolm greeted her cordially and she responded cordially. He just sat there looking at her. She had grave trouble holding his stare. She was the first to look away. He continued to look at her. She was now avoiding his gaze and had begun to fidget on her chair.

She asked for something to drink. He just gazed at her without responding. She repeated her request. When he didn't respond, she repeated her request with a demand that he at least acknowledge her request. He continued to gaze at her until a knock on the door. He rose, went to the door, listened to what was being said, then exited the room, making sure to make a show of locking the door.

Then the team watched her from the other side of the one way mirror. She was becoming more and more unnerved with the lack of communication, drink, or other accommodations. She began pacing around the room. When she started talking to herself, they started the tape. They left her there alone for the next two hours. During this time, they had left Gantry alone without food, drink, or other accommodations as well. They intended to leave him alone for much longer before they even attempted to speak with him.

Malcolm asked George if he was ready to eat. George still was not functioning too well, so Malcolm took him out to eat. Once George had had something to eat, he began to open up. George was now rattling quite profusely. When Malcolm felt he had allowed him enough leeway, he gave him a hearty slap. George stopped mid sentence. He just looked at Malcolm and then he thanked him. Malcolm just accepted it and stated it was time to go back and provide some more intimidation for Julia.

When they arrived back at FBI headquarters, George asked to take the lead. At first, Malcolm was a little leery of giving him that privilege. Yet, if George asked to do so, he may just be ready to take that step. George went into the room and motioned for Julia to sit down. Just as Malcolm had done, he stared at Julia daring her to maintain his gaze all the while not saying anything. In fact, he was actually beginning to enjoy her discomfort. So much so, he started to grin while she became more and more uncomfortable. He realized just how powerful silence could be. He continued to grin, gaze, and wait until she cracked. They had been at this a mere two hours after his supper when she lost it.

"What the hell do you want from me?"

Since his silence had been successful thus far, he decided to continue to sit and grin while waiting to see what else she might divulge without a single question. He didn't have long to wait. She had gotten up and started pacing, he took a cue from her and exited the room. This time his exit started a barrage of verbal retorts that might scar even a sailor's ear. Both he and Malcolm continued to wait. It wasn't' too much longer before she started ranting at the mirror.

"I didn't come up with all of this on my own...... Stanford was the entire reason that we were where we were…. I needed someone who could take care of getting us out of there without Stanford knowing that we weren't dead…."

"If Jasper hadn't brought Gantry to the house one night, I wouldn't have even come up with the explosion….."

An hour later, they had found out that Julia had wanted to leave Stanford taking the kids with her without Stanford being aware that it had occurred. Gantry had met Jasper at the treatment facility where he had befriended him. They had then started meeting each other after his release. They had went to Alysson's and Jessie's home where they began to perform at their best. They had slowly brought Catherine into the picture. It was only when Julia had approached Gantry about knowing someone who could perform the explosion in such a fashion to do the least damage to surrounding property while allowing her to disappear with the kids that she had been drawn into the picture a little more. She was appalled to see what her kids were doing for money, but needed that money to pay for the explosion. She had vowed to get them out of the life initially until she realized that they really liked the sickness of incest sexual intercourse and the attention that Alysson and Jessie were giving them. When Stanford kept pushing, Alysson couldn't stand it anymore and had torched her own garage to end his life. That meant they needed to escape and that meant their hideout in the mountains. Once there, she had lost control of the situation. She recognized that Gantry was the key person in the group and latched on to him to save herself. She had managed to do that as he had left a host of bodies with the assistance of Alysson, Jasper, and Catherine. She denied any culpability. She claimed she was along for the ride alone, not to perform any of the murders or mayhem. Since this was all taped without any written statement, they decided to approach Gantry to see what he would say.

Gantry having a past history and this was his stopping point for all past deeds, he kept quiet. When confronted with Julia's confession, he continued to be silent. That being said, Malcolm was satisfied that they had found the culprits and that they were going to prosecuted to the fullest extent of the law.

George was also satisfied. The hunt was over. The crime would and could be prosecuted. He was able to say that Carl's perseverance would be rewarded. Now, he could finally relax. He thanked Malcolm for all of his help, told him how sorry he was for all of the lives lost, and that he could be reached via the sheriff's office.

Malcolm thanked George as well. He also let him know that Carl's perseverance was the reason that this had not died with the initial explosion. He informed him that he would be glad to have him as part of any investigations in the future. That being said, it was time for them to try and return to the normalcy of their lives. George and Malcolm said their goodbyes and went their separate ways knowing that if they needed each other in the future, they could call upon each other in the future.